DELICATE REVENGE

A DARK SECRET SOCIETY ROMANCE

ALTA HENSLEY

STASIA BLACK

Special Thank you to our editor, Maggie Ryan, and our wonderful beta readers.

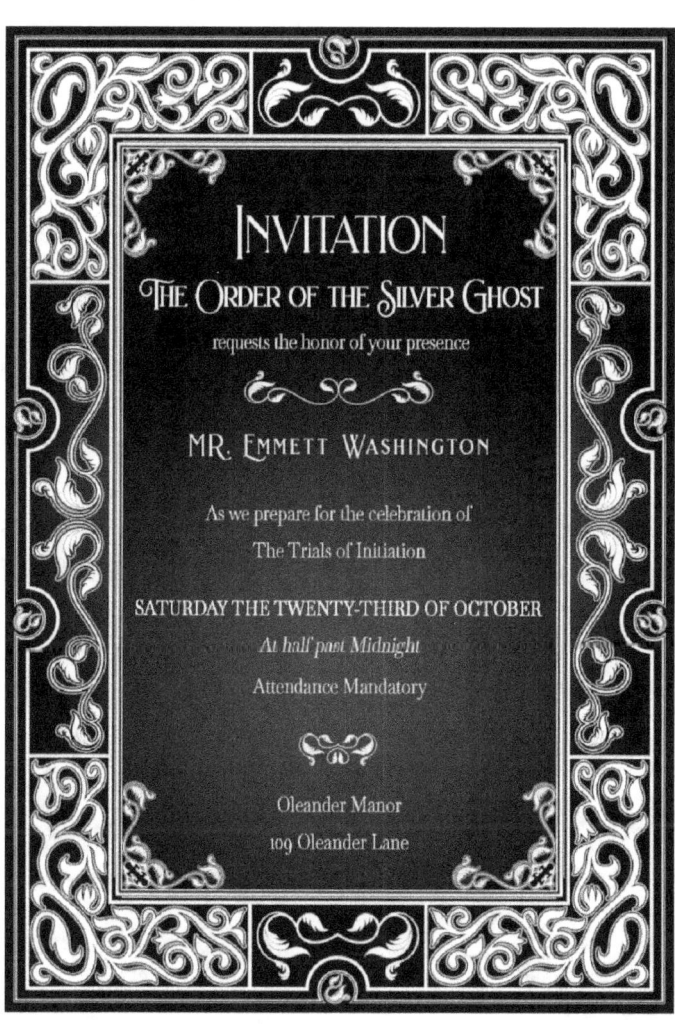

INVITATION

THE ORDER OF THE SILVER GHOST

requests the honor of your presence

MR. EMMETT WASHINGTON

As we prepare for the celebration of
The Trials of Initiation

SATURDAY THE TWENTY-THIRD OF OCTOBER

At half past Midnight

Attendance Mandatory

Oleander Manor

109 Oleander Lane

1

EMMETT

It was finally my turn.

I'd patiently watched all my friends from my recruit group be initiated into The Order of the Silver Ghost before me. Walker and I were the last to go, and I couldn't wait to get my time over with. It wasn't like I was overly anxious to be part of the Order for the same reasons that Montgomery or Beau were. I didn't grow up waiting for when I'd finally come of age. I wasn't bred for this like the men before me. There wasn't a speck of blue-blood in my veins. My father was the first in our family to be a member of the Order, and I would be the second.

Young blood.

Young money.

An outsider trying to belong to a secret society that rarely allowed newcomers in.

Though it would have been very hard for the Elders of the Order to deny my father access to their club full of the rich and powerful. They couldn't resist having him as part of their society when my father had more money in his pinky than some of them had combined. My family business, though not rich in history, was wealthy as fuck thanks to the world of technology, solar energy, and being on the cutting edge of the future. Our *new* money engulfed the meager millions these men touted. Therefore, we bought our way into their boys' club.

Were we treated differently?

Fuck yes, we were.

But my father earned his place and his respect, and now it was my turn to do the same.

Would I have to work harder than the other men in my recruit group to prove I deserved to become a member of the Order?

I thought that was a given, but I was up for the challenge. In fact, I welcomed it. I planned on showing every member of the Order just how much I belonged in this dark and twisted society that lived behind the haunted walls of Oleander Manor.

I knew I'd have Trials. I knew they weren't for the weak or the timid. And though most of the Trials were only viewed by the members, and I was only going off information I got from rumors and the tales my friends who went through them before me told, I couldn't help but be excited for my own opportunity. I had a thirst for the dirty, the depraved, and anything that pushed the limits.

Bring it.

I was ready.

And as the clock chimed and the canes of the silver-cloaked Elders banged on the white marble floor of the ballroom, my time had finally come.

I stood in my white tuxedo before a line of belles dressed in an assortment of colors and designs of custom-made ball gowns. Classic elegance, which I planned to sully pretty damn fast. Each woman looked so pure, so classy, so perfect. And yet... soon... if chosen... they would be anything but.

And I fucking loved that idea.

I already knew what I'd have to do from watching the men before me. I approached the belles with a black ribbon in my hand to choose the lucky girl who I'd spend the next 109 days breaking. So many choices, but I knew I needed to tear the pearl necklace off the neck of just one. But who?

Very slowly, I meandered my way down the line, not really having a type of woman I was looking for. I needed someone who would be strong and had the mental strength to handle all of what the Elders would throw our way. Each Belle I walked by who refused to make eye contact or who trembled slightly was quickly ruled out. I loved submissive women... but I wanted to be the man to make them that way. I wanted to tame the fire, not have it already smoldering when I arrived.

And then I saw her.

Though... I had to do a double take, because it didn't seem right.

Bellamy Carmichael?

What the fuck was *Bellamy Carmichael* doing in the Oleander? The belles were supposed to be from the "wrong side of the tracks," and Bellamy was anything but. I remembered her from Darlington Prep. The little rich girl, debutante, cheerleader, prom queen, and total bitch stood before me in a pink gown like the princess she believed herself to be.

Bellamy fucking Carmichael.

Her sea-blue eyes connected with mine the minute I stood before her. I knew she recognized me. I could see she knew exactly who I was, but other than her eyes, the rest of her face remained expressionless. Her shoulders were held back, her spine stiff, and I had to hand it to her years of pageant training to give her such posture and composure. A stiff breeze could knock some of the other belles down next to her, but not Bellamy.

Strong. She most certainly appeared to be.

I wanted to ask her why she was in the room. I wanted to ask *how* she became a Belle. But I also knew the rules—no talking.

I wanted to look behind me at Montgomery or any of the other men I went to school with and see if they saw what I did. Did they recognize Bellamy? It had been years since school, but she was still a Georgian Southern belle in our society. She mingled amongst us at the parties, at the dinners, at the high-class engagements, and yet, here she was in the pits of depravity now. Could this be a mistake? Surely, she knew what happened at the Oleander. She was no stranger to the tales of what went on under the veil of secrecy of The Order of the Silver Ghost. She knew exactly what would happen if I chose her....

So why was she standing before me with her shiny blonde hair, her pink glossy lips, and her perfect hourglass figure just begging for me to choose her as my Belle?

Oh my God... her mother. Her mother would absolutely die if she knew her precious daughter stood in the white ballroom of the Oleander. The thought forced a smirk to my lips. I sort of liked the thought of what a scandal this could cause. I'd be lying if I said I didn't like the idea of soiling this perfect vision of purity before me.

And then a twinge of inferiority hit my gut like a semi. Could I handle Bellamy? Was I worthy of having her as my Belle? It was Bellamy fucking Carmichael!

Just like in high school. She was the cool kid, and I was anything but. And I hated her for it. Silent rage quickly replaced my momentary lapse of confidence, and without thinking any further, I took hold of the pearls around her neck and snapped them off her flesh.

Yes, she would be my Belle, and I would take great pleasure in breaking her.

Revenge. A delicate revenge would be mine by the time we were done with the Initiation. Not necessarily a revenge on her, but a revenge on the past. I would make her pay for all the times I had wished she would turn my way and give me a second thought, and I would also use the strength she always possessed to cement my position into the Order.

Yes, Bellamy Carmichael would make the perfect Belle.

Tying the black ribbon into a bow around her neck, I heard, "Emmett Washington, have you chosen your Belle for the Initiation?"

I took a step back from Bellamy in her perfect princess dress that I'd soon be tearing off her and nodded. "I have chosen my Belle."

The sound of a loud banging cane and murmurs of the Order were the last things I heard as Bellamy and I were led out of the ballroom to the second-floor bedroom to consummate my decision. I knew what would be expected next.

Did Bellamy?

Did she know I was about to fuck her, with the Elders as our audience?

I glanced at her beside me and whispered, "Bellamy."

"Emmett," she replied simply, not turning her head to look at me.

"Is this what you want?" I had to ask. I had to know. "It's not too late to back out."

There were still belles downstairs entertaining the Elders... so I knew I could still choose another if she did completely chicken out. Now that reality could be slapping her in the face, I wanted to give her this last-minute chance to run with her bold but very naïve tail between her legs.

There was no way this little Southern belle knew what she was getting herself into. Not fully.

"I wouldn't be here if I didn't."

And there was the sassy Bellamy I remembered.

I wanted a full conversation, however—sassy or not. I wanted to look her straight in the eyes as we spoke. I had so many questions, and yet there was no time for any of it. I also didn't want to care why she was here. I didn't want to see her as anything more than a Belle I'd use to earn my place in the Order. The conflict of emotions made me wonder if I chose correctly. Maybe choosing a complete stranger would have been better... and yet the pearls had been broken, and the decision had been made. We were in motion, and nothing could stop the progression of the night.

As we entered the bedroom surrounded by antiques of ancestors not of my descent and furniture that held memories of family not belonging to me, I made a silent vow to not let this woman get in my head. I would not revert to the quiet and nerdy kid I was in school with a secret crush on the popular beauty who mastered the hallways of Darlington. I wouldn't allow myself to feel less-than. I wouldn't let her take over the power and control. No, I would not allow one ounce of my power to falter.

As if the Elders were reading my mind and felt the need to punctuate the end of my internal vow, they banged their canes and announced, "Let the consummation begin."

I gave Bellamy her chance to exit the scene, but she remained. So, at this point... game on.

We approached the bed, the Elders lined up at the foot of it, prepared to watch our every move. So fucked up, but it was a challenge I welcomed. If the fuckers wanted to watch me have sex with Bellamy, I planned to give them one hell of a show.

Not hesitating, I grasped Bellamy by the upper arm and spun her around so I could unzip her pretty pink ball gown. I couldn't wait another second to see if naked Bellamy lived up to my high-school fantasies.

The dress pooled at her feet, and though she had sexy white, lace lingerie underneath, I had zero patience to appreciate it before I spun her around to face me and shed her of every last bit of fabric remaining. I took a step back just so I could fully take in her beauty all for myself. Yes, Bellamy lived up to every damn fantasy I had... and then some. My dick hardened to a point of needing to remove my own clothing just so I could release some of the pressure. The entire time I did, Bellamy simply stood before me, though I caught her several times stealing uncomfortable looks at the Elders in the room.

Yes, my dear Bellamy, they are watching.

I could take this entire night slowly and really torture the girl, but my throbbing cock screamed to be inside her. Slow would have to happen another time, and the flicker of fear in her eyes did succeed at making me want to give her a little mercy. Just a little... since I could be a sadistic asshole at times. Especially in the bedroom.

Just as I was getting ready to pounce, Bellamy took it upon herself and bent over the bed, ass out, legs parted slightly so I could see the pink lips of her pussy just asking me to bury my dick in between them. Taking control—yes, that was exactly what she was doing. She was silently telling me to get it over with. Her nonverbal command warranted a punishment. She would soon learn that I didn't take orders from anyone, no matter how subtle or how incredibly sexy they were.

And I wasn't *that* merciful to just fuck her and be done.

"Roll over onto your back," I commanded as I approached. "You don't get to hide those tits of yours and your pussy from the sight of the Elders. I want them to see every inch of you on full display."

When she didn't move right away, I made first full contact with my palm on her ass, spanking her hard for her disobedience, and then flipped her over. Her eyes were glassy with tears of shame as her lips trembled. But when I lowered my fingertips to her pussy, I gave a devilish smile. My Southern belle was wet.

"What makes you wet, Belle? Is it all the eyes watching you be a very dirty girl, or knowing what's coming next?" I thrust my wet finger into her hole, causing her to gasp and arch her back.

She closed her eyes and bit her glossy lip.

"No, Bellamy. You keep those eyes open." I took both my hands at this point and pulled her pussy lips open, showing off her clit to those watching. "Just like we'll keep these lips of yours open. We all want to see just how wet you are."

Her eyes darted to the Elders and then back at me. I could see the "fuck you" dancing in the blue hues.

"You don't get to block this out. You don't get to hide." I released the spread but pushed my finger back inside her. I then added a second finger and pumped in and out, stretching her tight little hole as I did.

Her eyes closed, and she moaned loudly, which I couldn't help but love seeing, even though she was breaking my rule.

"Eyes open," I warned again, scissoring my fingers as I did so.

She obediently opened her eyes and locked them with mine. A single tear escaped from the corner. The droplet mixing with her mascara created a dark streak that ran down her face. The dirty line made my cock twitch in anticipation of seeing more.

"I like it when you cry, Bellamy. I like the dirty tears the most."

I also loved that she didn't try to close her legs or stop me from finger-fucking her in front of a roomful of observers. I, of course, couldn't read her mind, but I sure as hell could read her body, and the sexual juices coating my hand told me all I needed to know.

God, there was so much I wanted to do to her. There was so much I wanted to explore. I wanted to taste her. I wanted to see how her body would react to the arsenal of sexual acts I wanted to perform, but I also knew we would have 109 days to test every limit. For now, I needed to be inside her as much as I needed to take my next breath.

Replacing my fingers with my cock, I thrust inside her warmth with a loud groan. The primal urge to claim her took over every other sense inside me. Once I was balls-deep, I paused, took hold of her face, and turned her head to face the Elders.

"Watch them as I fuck you, Bellamy." I began thrusting in and out with an aggressive need to master her body. "I want you to get used to our audience. They're going to watch as I break you into my perfect submissive. They're going to watch me shatter that stubborn and spoiled debutante right out of you."

Her body rocked back and forth as I fucked her hard and deep. Her eyes remained open as I held her head in place, forcing her to face her shame and demons I knew she had to be battling. And whether my Belle liked it or not, she couldn't conceal the moans that escaped her parted lips. In and out, deeper and deeper, this woman would be mine.

Still not forgetting I had an audience and was giving a show, I kept my body off her torso so the Elders could see her perfect tits bounce with my every thrust. The bastards better had been secretly thanking me for the sight they were blessed to see. And Jesus fucking Christ... Bellamy was quite the sight. I chose wisely when it came to looks alone. The woman was everything I could have imagined and more. Big tits, full ass, smooth curves, and the tightest pussy I'd ever had.

The tightening around my cock and the soft cry from my Belle was all I needed to feel my own release erupt from the very depths of my core. My loud growl as I came was soon followed by the beating of a cane, reminding me of exactly where I was and what would come in the upcoming months. And though I was done for the moment... I had only sipped from the glass of debauchery. I had every intention of gulping from it next.

2

BELLAMY

As soon as the last Elder swished out of the room and the door closed behind them, I yanked the covers up over my breasts and glared at Emmett. "Was that entirely necessary?"

He stared coolly back at me. "What do you mean?"

I just gawked at him. I'd had a certain idea about how tonight would go.

I knew he'd pick me. Maybe I was full of myself to say so, but half the boys back in Darlington Prep had crushes on me. And Emmett, with his big puppy-dog eyes, hadn't been half as subtle as he thought.

Not that I cared.

Not back then.

I was too desperate, putting on the front as queen bee of the school. Everything perfect on the outside so no one ever thought to question anything going on behind closed doors.

And Emmett Washington had been nothing but an awkward tagalong to the *real* heirs who ran the school. He barely filled out the expensive clothes his new-money parents bought him.

But the Emmett who'd just slung me around and demanded such dirty things in the voice of a man who knew when he commanded things that people would obey.... Holy shit, where had he been hiding all this time?

I sat up straighter in bed so I could look down my nose at him—a trademark Carmichael move. "I *mean*, you didn't have to put on that performance for them." I flung my hand out toward the door. "It was unseemly. All we had to do was meet the requirements of having sex. You didn't have to turn it into a circus like that."

Emmett just smirked at me, making no move to cover himself at all. The girth of his cock had only slightly relaxed and was still obscenely large, lying against his thigh. "I don't think you get how this works, princess. I'm the one in charge here. You're *my* Belle. You do what I say."

I threw my hands up in the air. "But you picked someone who knows a little bit about how these things go. My mother lunches with all these men's wives, for God's sake! If I'd been a man, I'd be *in* the Order like my father was!"

His face lost the smirk, and he advanced toward me across the bed. "So why *are* you here? And why'd they let you in? I thought it was strictly off limits for—" He smirked again, looking me up and down as if finding something lacking. "—girls like you."

My chin jutted into the air. "You mean women with class?"

He glared. "I mean women who are too uppity to be grateful for the opportunity. Which it seems like you are. So tell me, Bellamy, did I make a mistake choosing you?"

I glared back at him. "You know you didn't." I allowed a little spite to enter my smile. "After all, I was there." I gestured beneath us at the bed. "You seemed to be pleased with your choice."

His eyes were cold and calculating as a snake as he smiled back. "So did you. Is that why you volunteered to be a Belle? So you could be fucked rough and dirty like a slut? I bet if I reached between your legs right now you'd still be slick for me to go again."

"You wish, you son of a bitch."

A finger came sharply into my face. "This is your first and only warning. You will refer to me as *Sir*."

I laughed. I couldn't help it. But really, he couldn't actually be serious.

But he wasn't laughing... or even smiling.

"I'm not fucking kidding," he clarified. "If we do this, we do this my way. Otherwise, you can walk your pretty pink little ass on down the stairs and out the door."

"But," I balked, "there's no part of the rules that say I have to call you—"

"These are my rules. And the rules say the Belle is to please her Initiate at all times."

For a second, my mouth just dropped open. I heard about these Trials for years in whispers and rumors, and I'd never heard about anything like this. "So what?" I asked. "You just want me to be your round-the-clock slave?"

The honest to God truth is that I should have run as soon as I saw the gleeful light enter his eyes at my question.

"That's exactly what it means," he said, not giving an inch.

"But—"

"No buts," he cut me off.

"That's not fair!" I cried.

He laughed at that, and it wasn't a kind or happy laugh. He just got close to me and took my chin in his hand. Not a painful grip, but it was firm.

"You think life is fair, princess?" He shook his head, and

his eyes had never been so dark. "Well, that's your first mistake. You think it was fair that you were born with everything, and someone like my mother was born with nothing? You think it's fair all the other women vying for your spot needed the prize that comes along with passing these Trials more than you ever could, but I picked you anyway? You think it's fair that people die of starvation and disease on this planet every single fucking day, but you *literally* eat with a silver spoon most days of your life?"

He'd been inching closer to my face with his every word, my chin still in his grip. "Wake up. You're about to get a crash course in fairness, princess. Because life isn't fucking fair."

I jerked back from his touch, and he just grinned.

"Why are you being so hateful?" I asked, wanting to shove him in the chest or punch him. I wanted to hurt him like he was hurting me with his words.

He thought he knew me because he'd seen me from afar for a few years in high school? Screw him. He didn't know me. None of them knew me.

"I'm not being hateful, princess."

I glared at him. "Stop fucking calling me that."

"Princess. I'll call you anything I fucking please. And you will obey me as your master, both when we're downstairs during Trials and the rest of the time."

He was nuts. He was seriously out of his damn mind if he thought—

"You're the one who showed up where she didn't belong tonight, *princess*. If you don't agree to the terms of my contract, all you have to do is walk down those stairs and leave."

Damn him.

Goddamn him.

He had me over a barrel, and he knew it, even if he didn't know the specifics.

I thought back to the wedding when I so foolishly came up with this plan. Okay, so none of this had really been my idea.

It was my mother's idea to whore me out to save the family fortune.

But *I* had foolishly chosen Emmett, thinking he'd be the easier of the last two bachelors left to tame.

Ha.

Hahahaha. Glaring at the black-eyed man in front of me, I'd sooner move a Mack truck than change the mind of this stubborn bastard who wanted me as his *slave.*

A slave? He was right on some accounts. I had grown up pampered, and what he was asking.... Well, actually what exactly *was* he asking for?

"What do you mean, a contract?" I asked. A good negotiator never made a decision before they had all the facts.

"We discuss soft and hard limits, what you are and aren't willing to do. I'll outline my expectations of you in this power exchange."

His tone had changed completely, as if he were a lawyer discussing clauses in a business meeting. "If there's anything you're absolutely unwilling to do, sexually or otherwise, we talk through it and negotiate. You'll have a safeword that will stop all play if you feel things have gone too far beyond your comfort zone. But in this situation, and unlike a true BDSM dynamic, using your safeword will mean exiting the mansion and leaving the Trials early, thus failing."

I could only sit there blinking for several moments.

"Why would you make the Trials harder than they already are? Don't you want to pass and become a member of the Silver Ghost?"

Emmett just shrugged. "Yes, I do. But I want it on my terms. Part of signing a contract like this is building trust with my submissive. I should never push you so hard you'd ever have to use your safeword. But I *will* push you. I intend to show the Elders that I am all they're looking for in an Initiate and more. And I will demonstrate that through you."

I let out a heavy breath. Good Lord, what had I gotten myself into?

But before I could think much more about it, Emmett stood up, naked as the day he was born and, I had to grudgingly admit, as gloriously handsome as a god—all hard muscle and tight ass.

I yanked my eyes away before he caught me staring. Soon, he returned to bed, and he had actual paperwork. He wasn't kidding about the contract.

It wasn't just a page or two either. It was a bound packet. With a table of contents.

I was wide-eyed as Emmett sat down beside me and started flipping through the contents and reading over it in the same lawyer voice as before.

Terms. Goals. The Rights and Responsibilities of the Master.

But it was when we got to the Responsibilities and Availability of the Slave that things *really* got interesting. The slave was always to be available to the Master in the arrangement Emmett was proposing—a twenty-four seven power exchange. I gulped even at the thought. Could I do it? Give over control of my life, every minute of it, for three months?

It was basically what I thought I was signing up for anyway; I just assumed I'd have some time to myself in the room. A little downtime here and there.

But maybe this way would be better. Wouldn't it be... interesting, if not a little refreshing, to not have to worry about *anything* for three months? To have someone else making all the decisions and taking on all the responsibilities for a while.

Then I narrowed my eyes at Emmett.

Who continued to read through the list of sexual positions, toys, and kinks—some of which made my eyes pop open.

I immediately struck through the idea of fisting. No, no thank you. Moving on.

He rolled his eyes but didn't press the point. Good Lord, did he actually—

Nope, not going to think about it. Moving on, moving on.

I had to ask him about several other terms, each more eye-opening than the last. I'd always thought myself a fairly open person when it came to sex, but compared to the things he was describing, I felt like the naive small-town girl I was.

I didn't like it.

And I certainly didn't like it when we got to the section labeled **Punishment**.

"Um, excuse me?" I asked. "Punishment? I'm not a child."

He just arched an eyebrow. "Submissives who exhibit bratty behavior get punished."

"Bratty behav—" I cut off, already feeling the heat rise in my cheeks.

"Talking back. Not obeying quickly enough. Trying my patience. Failing to live up to my exacting standards."

I rolled my eyes at him, and he reached forward, grabbing me tight by the nape of my neck so that I was forced to look at him eye-to-eye, nose-to-nose. "Rolling your eyes," he said in a low growl that for some ridiculous reason made my nipples harden.

I wanted to shove him away, but I didn't. I just clenched my jaw and asked through my teeth, "And what will these *punishments* entail?"

A truly wicked grin crossed his face at the question. "Oh, you'll see, princess. You'll see. Now are you signing the contract or walking out the door right now?" He held out a pen he'd magically produced from somewhere.

I swallowed and then breathed out as quietly as I could.

I had no choice.

I grabbed the pen out of his hand and signed the line on the last page beside where he'd written out my name in neat script.

Why did I have the feeling that I'd just signed my life, dignity, and entire future away?

3

EMMETT

I 've always been a sucker for a submissive in bed in the morning. Tousled hair, smeared makeup, and the distant smell of sex from the night before were my addictive drug. But not this morning. I kept my hands off Bellamy... for now. We'd have plenty of time to make up for it tonight, no doubt, but this morning was more about watching, learning, studying every move she made so I'd know just how to handle her in the future.

First thing I noticed... she was shy. At least when it came to her body and appearance. Her subtle movements to try to conceal her nudity first thing in the morning from my waking eyes weren't lost on me. She wasn't *made up* like the perfect Barbie doll, and her natural beauty clearly made her uncomfortable. The minute she exited the bathroom after a ridiculously long shower and whatever else she did behind the closed door, I instantly noticed a renewed confidence about her. Almost as if she had her war paint on and was now prepared for battle.

I also remembered her always being very sociable and chatty. The woman knew how to work a room at a party like a true southern socialite. But this morning, she remained very quiet. She spoke few words to me and seemed to just watch my every move. No doubt she was studying me as I was her.

As we sat down in the formal dining room, sitting across from each other at the extremely long table, we both stared each other down while we waited for Mrs. H to come in with our breakfast.

"Did you sleep well?" I began, feeling as if she was waiting for me to say the first word.

"No," she stated simply, still locking her eyes with me. "I don't see how I could, considering we were sharing a bed together—naked per your orders."

"I could have tied you up or had you sleep at my feet. I could have even had a cage brought in and had you sleep inside as my little pet," I countered with an evil grin. "So, consider yourself lucky and be grateful for the ability to sleep in the bed with my only expectation being that you remain naked."

She didn't say another word but simply scowled in my direction.

Clearly, this would be a battle of wills. I could see the sizzle beneath the blue in her eyes. This woman would be a challenge, but something about the idea made my cock twitch.

Mrs. H entered and gave both of us a warm smile. "What can I get you two for breakfast?"

"I will have scrambled eggs, toast, and a bowl of fruit," I said. "And black coffee, please."

Mrs. H nodded and then looked at Bellamy. "And for you?"

"She'll have the same as me," I ordered for her.

Bellamy shot daggers from her eyes at me as her mouth

opened to order for herself. "I'll just have coffee and some fruit," she snapped, giving me the nastiest look she could muster.

"She'll have exactly what I'm having," I restated, narrowing my eyes and locking my jaw as I did so. I didn't like to be challenged, especially in front of someone else.

Mrs. H looked at me and shook her head. "Emmett, can we save the dominance for the Trials, please?"

"She will have exactly what I ordered. Final."

Bellamy shifted in her seat, and I could tell the glare I gave her made her uncomfortable. Which was a good thing. It meant she had some common sense and knew she pushed me with her stubborn act.

"I'll have what he's having," Bellamy finally said in a softer voice, but she stiffened her spine and lifted her chin as if that was giving her some sort of secret power.

Mrs. H smirked and shook her head. "You two better get this shit figured out. I'm not going to be part of your games every mealtime." She turned to me and pointed. "And don't you think for one second you can boss *me* around."

I gave her a toothy smile and nodded. "I would never think such a thing. Thank you, Mrs. H."

When she left to get our breakfast, I took a deep breath and allowed the heaviness in the air to weigh down upon Bellamy. Maybe she expected me to chastise her or even yell, because her body tensed. My look said it all; I knew I had the ability to break down the strongest person in the boardroom with the intensity I could exude. And by how uneasy Bellamy appeared, my silence was only making the tension at the table worsen.

"I didn't want eggs or toast," she finally said.

"I didn't ask."

"I don't need you to order for me."

I leaned back in my chair and crossed my arms against my chest. "Take your panties off," I commanded in a firm but calm voice.

Her eyes widened; her mouth opened, closed, and then opened again. "Excuse me?"

"I said for you to take off your panties."

Her eyes darted to the door Mrs. H had just exited and then back at me. "Why in the world would I do that?"

"Bellamy," I said with warning laced thickly in the syllables of her name. "I will tell you one more time. Remove your panties, now. If you fail to do as I ask, I will get up, march over there, and remove them myself. But if I have to get out of this chair and do so, there will be consequences."

Pink tinged her cheeks as she nibbled the corner of her mouth. "Emmett, is this really necessary?" I began to stand, but she quickly motioned for me to stay seated. "Okay, okay," she quickly snapped.

Glancing at the door one more time, she then reached beneath the table, hiked up her dress, and pulled her lace panties down to her ankles. She bent down and removed them as I'd ordered.

Lifting up and dangling them off her index finger, she asked, "And what would you like me to do with them now, almighty Master?"

Her renewed courage and sass made it very hard not to chuckle, but I clenched my jaw to control the urge.

"Set them next to your napkin on the table. They'll sit there throughout breakfast to remind you to behave. I don't tolerate being questioned in front of others. If I want to order for you, if I want to oversee the care for my submissive, and if I want to be the one in charge of what happens to you at every waking moment of the day, I will. Are we clear?"

She placed the panties down, but I could see she wasn't happy—not one single bit.

"Am I clear?" I asked again forcefully. I could see I might have to have a session with her very soon to teach her exactly what happened if she tested the limits with me.

"Yes," she finally said, her eyes silently telling me to go fuck myself as she did so.

"Yes, what?" I pressed, not paying attention to the defiance she clearly struggled to hold back.

"Yes, *sir*," she bit out just as Mrs. H reentered the room with much-needed coffee.

When Mrs. H saw the panties on the table, she shook her head but didn't say a single word. She silently left to go get the rest of our breakfast.

"Is embarrassing me part of this?" Bellamy asked.

"If needed," I answered. "You clearly have been spoiled your entire life. You've never had someone tell you no or take you in hand."

"Take me in hand? What exactly does that mean?"

I chuckled as I sipped from my coffee. "Oh, you'll soon find out. Trust me on that."

"And you don't know me," she countered as she crossed her arms over her chest, not drinking from her coffee—as if it was somehow tainted, because I ordered it for her. "You can sit there and assume you do, but you have no idea what kind of life I lived or am living now."

"I'm going off fact," I stated. "Not only do I remember you as the spoiled little rich girl at Darlington Prep, but I've also watched you flutter around from party to party and from one wealthy man to another, trying to land Mr. Rich and Powerful."

She couldn't hide the sneer on her face. I pissed her off, but I supposed that was what happened when she wasn't used to having someone tell her the truth. Being surrounded by yes people her entire life had polished her up like a diamond but then made her unable to see the flaws.

Once upon a time, I'd been unable to see those flaws too. I'd been too dazzled by the sparkle, just like everyone else. I hadn't grown up in the Darlington Prep school system from birth like all the other kids. I was a transplant in eighth grade from California. We hadn't always been rich, but Dad struck it bigtime by building his business from the ground up.

He started with solar and expanded from there into electric cars, and the sky was the limit after that. Literally. We were building rockets now, joining in the space race. He was just less ostentatious than some of the other billionaire assholes out there and not as interested in media spotlight.

But back when we first moved here, he was just amassing his power and beginning to get into electric cars. That was why he'd moved. He'd built a factory outside of Atlanta. The Order of Silver Ghosts had barely even let him in, and it was only because he'd made a massive donation to the society that they agreed.

Fitting in had been just as hard for me. Montgomery and the other guys let me into their group, but I was undeniably an outsider. I was a skinny kid from California whose voice hadn't even dropped yet. I liked math more than watching football or playing video games. I was a hang-along, but we all did a good enough job pretending that I wasn't so I could mostly forget that it was only my father's money that had effectively bought me these friendships.

Except when it came to Bellamy Carmichael. She was beautiful, popular, the girl every other girl wanted to be and every guy wanted to fuck. And she was just as untouchable.

She only dated seniors, and when we were finally seniors, she dated college guys. She certainly never gave any of the guys in our school the time of day, though she did hang around with my friend group.

By the time we got to high school, the guys and I felt more like genuine friends. I'd accepted the five of them would always be closer to each other than they would be with me. It was inevitable, them all having grown up together since the damn cradle. I'd grown into my lanky frame a little, and I even dated here and there.

It was after Dad landed the contract with NASA and I was feeling more secure than ever that I finally got up the nerve to talk to her. Bellamy. The goddess I'd worshipped from afar for five years. She sat at the table with us every single day and never said a word to me. To be fair, I never talked to her either.

But this was my time.

SHE'D JUST GONE ON AT LENGTH THE WEEK BEFORE ABOUT breaking up with her most recent boyfriend. And prom was three weeks away.

It was now or never.

After the bell rang signaling the end of lunch, I left my tray on the table and hurried around to intersect Bellamy before she could escape to her next class. "Hey, Bellamy," I said, then swallowed hard. Jesus, why was my voice suddenly so dry? I could hear my heart pounding in my ears.

She stopped, frowning at me in her path and pulling out her phone to check her texts.

"Wannagotothedance?"

"Huh?" She looked up at me from her phone.

I coughed a little, clearing my throat. "The dance. Um. Prom. Wanna go? With, um... me?"

She turned her head, looking around us, eyes wide. Several people were watching on. Shit. I hadn't intended on having an audience. This was just where I knew I could catch her every day.

I opened my mouth to say something else, maybe to apologize for asking her like this, or to tell her how long I'd liked her and that I'd like to get to know her better. That I saw her. How, yes, most of the time she was smiling and putting on such a great show for everyone, but I saw how sometimes she looked sad and lost when she didn't think anyone was looking.

I wanted to tell her that I got that, that I felt like that too sometimes. Yeah, my dad was super successful, but I barely knew him, because he was gone so often.

But whatever I might have said was cut off by her caustic laugh once her eyes finally came back to me.

"Go to the prom? With you?" She said it so loud that people who hadn't been stopping to look before did now. Like they did at car crashes.

And that was what it felt like. Her words hit me like a semi-truck as her beautiful features turned cruel. I wish I could say she was ugly in that moment, but no; even as she cut me into pieces, she was gorgeous.

"My grandmother was best friends with the Rockefellers." She snorted, then pointed behind me. "You know they only put up with you because of your rich daddy, right? You aren't a blueblood."

"Jesus, you don't have to be a bitch, Bellamy," Montgomery said from behind me, and I felt my face go red from my friend having to defend me.

Bellamy only shifted and shrugged. "Sorry if I'm the only one who will tell it like it really is." Then she turned and flounced away from us, all like she hadn't just dug a knife right in the center of my chest.

"HIGH SCHOOL WAS A LONG TIME AGO," SHE SAID, BRINGING ME back to the present. "I don't live in the past. The girl I was then is most certainly not the woman I am now. Just as I hope the *boy* you were, sitting in the lunchroom and gawking at me every day, is not the man sitting across from me now. And as for my life now... if I remember correctly, you were at the exact same Darlington socials surrounded by women who wanted you to be their sugar daddy. So don't sit and judge me, unless you can do the same to yourself. We both play the game, Emmett. It's Darlington. It's who and what we are."

After high school, I left for college, determined to become my own man. No one would ever look down on me the way she had that day. They could try, but I learned my own worth and place in the world while I was away. And then I came back to Darlington to claim the place that was deservedly mine.

My palm itched to smack that pantiless ass of hers to show her exactly the *man* I'd grown to be. Fortunately for Bellamy, Mrs. H entered with our breakfast.

As if Mrs. H could sense the tension in the room, she quickly served the meal and then walked over to an armoire, pulled out a white box with a black ribbon, and placed it on the table in front of Bellamy. "It's for tonight's Trial. Every night before a Trial, you will get a box with what you are both to wear" was all she said before leaving us.

"Should we see what's inside?" Bellamy asked as she fingered the black ribbon on the box.

"Go ahead and open it." I took a deep breath, needing

the distraction to regain my control. Bellamy definitely had a way of getting under my skin, but I refused to allow her to see just how much.

She pulled out a tuxedo for me, which I figured as much, and then she stared into an almost empty box. All that remained was a paint brush and a pair of silver high heels.

She held the paintbrush and lifted an eyebrow as she asked, "I'm assuming this is all I get?"

I took my first bite of food and swallowed down the deep laughter that wanted to escape. "Looks that way." I nodded to her plate. "Eat all your breakfast. I'm not asking. I'm not suggesting. I'm telling."

I paused, waiting for some sort of snarky response. I was prepared to get up, remove my belt, and teach Bellamy exactly what happened if she disobeyed me, but I'd much rather save it for when my belly wasn't growling and the coffee had time to kick in. Luckily for me, Bellamy wasn't in the mood for a battle quite yet. Though I saw her nostrils flare slightly, and I could see she was grinding her perfect white teeth, she remained quiet and dug into her meal.

"Bellamy," I finally said, cutting into the silence of our eating after several moments. "About tonight. I want you to know I have some expectations for the Trials."

She looked at me mid-chew but didn't say anything.

"I want there to be no mistake. There will be a lot of men at the Trials. All eyes will be on you, but there is one rule I will never allow you to break. You are *mine*. Only mine. You will not touch another, speak with another, or even look at another man unless I give you permission to do so. *Mine*. Are we clear?"

She nodded as she swallowed the toast, needing to sip from the coffee to help wash it down.

"I also expect perfection. I want our Trial to be better

than any of the Initiates before us and even those who follow. I don't do mediocre. I never have. If the Elders want a show, we will give it to them. If they demand we do anything... we do it. I don't want them to see sass, to see resistance, or any other kind of disrespect. And with that said, I want you to know that I will always protect you, care for you, and guide you through the entire process. You are mine, and I don't take that responsibility lightly. I don't just demand your respect, but you will soon see that I'll earn it every step of the way. Yet I need you to allow me to lead. I need you to submit and trust. Are we clear in that?"

"Yes," she squeaked out. "Yes, *sir*." She placed her fork down and leaned forward to give emphasis on her next words. "I want to pass these Trials just as much as you do. And like you... I don't do mediocre. I've been groomed my entire life to be perfect. You are about to see just how perfect I can be at what the Order throws our way."

4

BELLAMY

Apparently, *perfection* meant walking down the elegant stairwell of the Oleander naked as a jaybird—oh, except for the silver Louboutin heels. I held my head high and my back straight, just like we learned in Cotillion classes all those years ago. Granted, I didn't think they had a scenario like *this* in mind back when Mrs. Marshall was instructing us in the squeaky high-pitched voice about "manners" and "breeding" and how they'd "impact our marriageability."

Sometimes, it felt like Darlington County had been left back in the 20th century... or on a night like tonight as I descended into an exquisite white-marbled den of sin lit by a gas chandelier, like the 19th.

Other naked women walked in as I entered the ball-room. Men in tuxes and silver robes waited for us. My eyes widened slightly when I passed by a group of faces I recognized—Montgomery Kingston and his friends Beau and Rafe. Shit, I was prancing around naked in front of people I *knew*. When Emmett had fucked me so enthusiastically, at least it had only been in front of the Elders, but tonight... tonight would be in front of everyone.

Beside me, Emmett didn't so much as hold out an arm to steady me. No, every bit of this was a test, to see if I would stand on my own two feet. He wouldn't coddle me, not one bit. He thought I was a spoiled brat as it was.

Everyone was almost gathered when Emmett finally leaned over. I thought he might offer some encouragement after all. But I was soon proven wrong when he whispered low and in that commanding voice of his, "Just a reminder, you are *mine*. You are not allowed to make eye contact with any other man in the room tonight. Only me. You are not allowed to *touch* any man. Only me. And remember, I expect perfection."

I nodded, half listening. If all he was going to do was order me around right before we were supposed to be on stage, he could go fuck himself. I needed to focus. He'd told me I needed to be perfect tonight. Well, things were starting to happen, and I couldn't afford to miss a single detail.

One of the Elders stood in the center of the room and banged his cane once we'd all arranged ourselves. The doors the girls had entered through shut behind them ominously. In the corner, two violinists stood. One violin began, striking a slow, long, vibrating note. Then the second joined in, a searing note so that when the two instruments sang together, the song pulsated right through you.

I gasped a little, looking around to see if other people were affected or if it was the signal for something.

But the Elder with the cane in the center of the room spoke up again as the two violins continued to dance and entwine their music with one another, sensually promising what was to come.

"Women, bring forth your paint pots. Dance and paint one another for the delight of our eyes."

I looked around and saw that half the women held little earthen pots full of silver paint. It was then that I finally realized what was different about the ballroom. The floor had been covered in panels that locked together to protect the marble floor. They'd prepared for things to get messy.

Those with pots paired up with those of us without. The music became more intense as the woman with shiny black hair reached her small, delicate hand into the pot and came out with fingers dripping silver.

Shit, there was nothing to do but pretend I didn't know anyone here. I couldn't think about Montgomery or any of the other guys I'd grown up with.

I took a bold step forward to the woman, and she smiled. I didn't have to look behind me to know Emmett's eyes were laser-focused on me. But he needn't have worried. I'd gotten his message loud and clear.

Perfection. I'd put on a show for him. For all of them. Let them look.

I was Bellamy goddamned Carmichael, for Christ's sake. I was no shrinking daisy. If we were to be objectified, well, I'd show I was the most desirable object in the room. I would revel in their stares. They would give me power. I'd feed off them like I always had.

So I arched my chest toward the raven-haired beauty. Her dripping silver hand landed on my breast. She wasn't shy about massaging the paint into my skin, rubbing her thumb over my areola and puckered nipple.

I hissed from the cool of the paint and because I knew Emmett would be watching my every reaction.

Fortune favored the bold, right? So I reached my hand in her pot, shivering when my hand dipped into the paint. I pulled out my sopping hand and reached toward the woman. I slid my hand up her sternum, leaving streaks of silver in my wake. Then I curved my hand up to her throat and back around her neck, tugging her head down until her lips were inches away from mine.

Daringly, I slid my eyes over to the sidelines where Emmett stood, glass of brandy in hand, watching me just like I thought he'd be. I smiled at him as I slid my tongue out of my mouth and teased her lips open, then kissed her. And I didn't miss the way he readjusted his stance and took a swallow of liquid.

My new friend was happy to play the game I was introducing. She gathered more paint and left a silver-handprint on my ass as she pulled my body into hers. She was all softness and curves in my palms.

Murmurs from the men on the sides of the room told us they liked the show we were giving them. I pulled away from the woman sharply. Getting fresh paint, I grabbed her plump breasts, then traced down to her belly button. Emmett said he wanted us to stand out from any other pair before us. So I would put on a show. And knowing his eyes were on me, I couldn't say that everything happening right now wasn't turning me the hell on.

After another dip in the pot, I reached between her thighs and pulled them open, forcing her legs farther apart. Silver paint dripped down the inside of her legs.

In return, she grabbed both of my ass cheeks, plumping them in her hand and then giving them a wet *smack* with her silver hands. Then she luxuriated in rubbing the paint around, up my back, and then down my ass crack.

Whistles and catcalls from the sidelines increased in volume until finally canes began to pound.

I lifted my eyes and looked around. The other women

were covered in paint just like me and my companion, and the men were clearly losing their shit they were so anxious to touch us and join in on the debauchery. Some already had their cocks out, fluffing them in preparation.

It was only then that I remembered, shit, Montgomery, Beau, and Rafe had seen everything I'd just done. I looked around the room, thankfully not seeing them. But I did catch sight of other men watching me lustfully as they banged their canes.

Only once the canes stopped banging and the Elder who'd spoken earlier walked to the center did I look back toward Emmett and meet his gaze... and saw that he looked pissed.

I looked to the floor, feeling my cheeks heat as I belatedly remembered the other part of the orders he'd hurriedly hissed at me before the orgy began—that I wasn't supposed to look at anyone else besides him. Shit.

But he couldn't have been serious about that. I couldn't control where my eyes went! Well, mostly, I'd just forgotten about it. But, Jesus, did the man seriously think he could control even my eye movement? That took control-freak to a whole new level. There was so much going on in the room; no one could blame me for being curious.

I'd missed whatever the Elder said after the canes stopped banging. Dammit. But there was no missing what I was supposed to do when Emmett came stalking toward me, demanding through his teeth once he reached me, "Knees."

All the other girls were dropping to their knees as men from the crowd came forward and chose silver-painted women at will. I hurriedly got to my knees as Emmett whipped out his tremendous, throbbing cock and presented it to my face. He couldn't be too mad at me if he was that turned on, right? Well, I knew one surefire way to ease any anger he might be feeling.

I cupped his balls with my right hand. The paint was mostly dry, but it still left a silver dusting on his heavy sac. I played with his balls as I lowered my head to his cock, toying with it with the tip of my tongue.

The shudder that went through his body at my touch was gratifying as hell. He tried to act like Mr. High and Mighty, but one swipe of my tongue and I had him on the edge. His cock throbbed in my mouth.

I barely remembered him from high school if I was being honest—it was probably bitchy to admit, but I'd never claimed to be a saint back then... or now. I grazed my teeth along his shaft before covering them back up with my lips and bobbing up and down over his tip repeatedly. I looked up at him and didn't miss the way his jaw clenched.

Whatever he'd been then, he was all man now. But when he looked down at me with my mouth stuffed so full of his cock that my eyes watered, what did he see? The queen bee who'd won Teen Miss Darlington County two times, both my sophomore and senior year? Did he see only the siren from moments ago, just another beautiful blonde covered in silver paint? Did he just see a woman to dominate, and anyone who'd play his kinky games would do?

I squeezed his balls, and his right hand came to my hair, his left hand to my wrist, pulling it away from his sac. Then he started to guide the pace at which I bobbed on and off him until finally he held the sides of my head in his hands. "You're going to take what I give you, and it's going to make you wet," he said.

I blinked, unsure at this turn of events. When I gave guys a blowjob, I was always the one in control. But here again, Emmett was flipping the tables on me.

"Touch yourself, but don't you dare fucking come," he commanded as he began to feed his cock back into my mouth. "And eyes on me."

I blinked and nodded, mouth full of his thick flesh. I reached down between my legs.

"Stick two fingers inside your cunt," he ordered as he started to really fuck my face. I did what he said. I *was* wet, which surprised me. I'd never been spoken to so crudely. And yet, the more crudely he spoke and used my body, the wetter I became.

"Fuck yourself with your fingers while I fuck your face," he said through panted breaths, his cock ridiculously large in my mouth. It was work to keep my lips covering my teeth. "And don't stop sucking me," he added. "I wanna feel that fucking vacuum mouth."

I nodded, trying to give him everything he was asking for, but it was overwhelming. I suckled as hard as I could while his cock was in my mouth, but he was relentless. I could only just catch my breath before he was coming at me again. And then working my own fingers inside myself and fighting my rising pleasure. Around us, canes continued to pound, along with men's groans and grunts of pleasure.

But it was impossible to look at anyone but up at Emmett, past his clenched torso and into those eyes that blazed down at me. "I'm coming. Don't lose a single drop. And don't stop fucking yourself."

He slowed down the frantic thrust of his hips as he pushed in one last time, and I sucked harder than ever, swirling all around his dick until the salt of his cum sprayed my tongue and the back of my throat.

I swallowed convulsively, and when some slipped out the edge of my mouth, I licked it up frantically, the same as I did some that spilled down the side of his shaft. And as I did, I couldn't help it.

I fucking came. Quick, fast, sharp.

I was licking up his balls, and I froze as my body spasmed. I breathed out and continued cleaning him with my tongue, hoping he hadn't noticed.

But when I glanced up and saw the furious fire in his eyes, I knew he had.

"Room," he ordered through his teeth. "Now."

Oh shit.

I looked around. We'd passed the Trial. I'd done good. Surely, that had to count for something. I got to my feet, a little unsteady at first in my heels, but Emmett again didn't even hold out an arm. So I steadied my damn self, held my head up high, and marched out of the room with the dignity of the Carmichael blood flowing through my veins.

5

EMMETT

"You know a punishment is coming, don't you?" I asked, fighting back the primal growl that wanted to unleash from deep inside.

She opened her mouth but quickly shut it. Instead, she simply nodded in response.

"I gave you clear instructions twice. And twice, you ignored them." I tilted her chin with my fingers so her gaze locked directly with mine.

She nodded once again, but the clench of her jaw told me she resisted the urge to retort something sassy back. At least she was smart enough to remain silent; although, in mere moments, she wouldn't be able to keep quiet no matter how hard she tried.

"You're going to learn tonight that when I give you a command, I expect it to be followed."

Her eyes narrowed, and the corner of her mouth twitched, but she didn't tell me to go fuck myself like I knew she wanted to.

"You are mine, Bellamy. As long as you reside in the Oleander, you are mine and only mine. Every single action of yours will reflect that. I saw you look at the other men—"

"Not in any sexual way," she finally cut in. "This isn't fair. I didn't do anything wrong. Not truly."

"But regardless, you looked at another man. At other *men*." I pulled her into the room fully and shut the door. Then, not giving her an option, I took her by the arm and led her closer to the bed. "I also told you not to come."

"I can't control my body like that simply because you *tell* me. It's not like I can or cannot come on command," she snapped. "This isn't some porno where the man says come, and the woman instantly does—or doesn't, in my case. This isn't fair!"

"You'll learn," I said, giving her a devilish smirk.

Oh yes, she'd learn.

Bellamy fought for breath as I kicked her legs wider with my feet and then slapped her pussy as a very small peek at what was to come.

A very small peek.

I then cupped her breasts, causing Bellamy's whimpers to fill the air.

"And you'll learn to beg to come after I spank that tight ass of yours. You'll plead for me to press my cock into you, making you scream my name," I stated sensually, my voice tight and rough.

She trembled, her body shuddering, no doubt with the thought of what was to come.

Bellamy cried out, losing any control she tried to keep hold of as I plunged two thick fingers deep inside her hungry pussy. Raking across her clit with my thumb, I twisted my fingers inside. Pulling her orgasm to the surface, Bellamy rocked her body against my hand.

"You're so wet for me. The thought of a punishment

coming is making your body come alive. It makes me think you acted out on purpose. Maybe you want your ass spanked? Maybe you want me to punish that little asshole of yours? Maybe this was your plan all along?"

She shook her head, but her breathing increased, and I felt the walls of her pussy tighten around my fingers. Not giving her the release she so desperately wanted, I removed my fingers as abruptly as I put them inside her.

I then walked over to the nightstand and pulled out a black box I had arranged to be delivered. It was waiting for me for when this occasion would occur. I placed it on the bed, took off my belt, and also laid it on the mattress, noticing Bellamy watched my every move as I sat down on the bed.

"Come here." I patted my lap so it was very clear what I expected. "Lie over my knee."

Her eyes widened, and her mouth opened to protest, but there must have been something in the way I looked at her, because the minute her eyes locked with mine, she did exactly as I ordered, pressing her bare stomach onto my lap and spreading her naked self across me.

Bellamy released a light gasp as I nudged her thighs apart with the press of my hand. Her upturned ass was now in the perfect position.

She looked over her shoulder at me, and I could see a mixture of uncertainty and arousal in her eyes. My guess was that Miss Bellamy had never been in this kind of situation in her life and wasn't sure what would come next.

I ran my palm from the top of her ass to where her butt met her thighs. "I'm going to spank this ass of yours."

Bellamy tensed, but she didn't move, wriggle, or fight my caress. I expected more of a battle but was pleased she didn't struggle. There was a submissive hidden behind all her attitude, and it might not take me nearly as long to break the wall of resistance as I thought. Though, part of her compliance was due to the fact that she had no idea what was coming.

Naivety tamed the beast.

It seemed her natural curiosity helped in her not fleeing and me having to restrain her—which I would've been more than willing to do.

I parted her legs farther, opening her crevice completely to my view. With only a breathy gasp and a slight tensing of her body, Bellamy allowed me to do as I pleased.

For now.

The pain on her ass and the humiliation from the discipline hadn't come yet, and when it did... no doubt, she wouldn't be as compliant to the punishment I'd bring down upon her.

My fingertip dipped into the natural contours of her bottom, sliding seductively along her puckered opening. "I'm not going to just spank this ass; I'm going to punish this tight hole as well." My finger rubbed over her anus in small measured circles.

Bellamy's breath caught, likely trapped in her throat by the news I just gave her.

I removed my hand and reached for the black box. She kept her face forward, clenching her fists as they dangled in front of her.

Moments later, I applied lubrication I pulled from the box to her puckered hole that I desperately craved to invade. I continued to rub and tease by pressing the tip of my fingertip past the tight skin.

Bellamy finally looked back over her shoulder, brushing the blonde locks from her eyes so she could see what I had in store.

"What is that?" she asked as she noticed what I pulled out of the box next.

"This is called a butt plug." I couldn't fight back the mischievous smile that washed across my face. "It's going to spread your hole and eventually get it ready for my cock."

I placed my hand between Bellamy's shoulder blades and pressed her all the way down again. The only thing she could see was the wooden floorboards below her. She had seen enough. She knew exactly how big the plug was and now knew what exactly it was that would be biting at her delicate hole.

She bucked against the metal plug as it made contact with her skin. "I've never had anything go inside.... My ass has always been off limits."

"Nothing is off limits to me. You should have put it on your list when we did the contract, and since you didn't... it's all mine to do with as I please."

I spread her cheeks and pressed the plug past the tight ring. She jerked and released a yelp as I slowly broke the barrier.

"Hold still," I ordered.

She whimpered at the sharp bite of the intrusion.

"Relax." I continued to press the plug farther, demanding access. "I want you to close your eyes and concentrate on the sensations."

She shook her head from side to side and tried to get off my lap, but I only held her more firmly in place. "That's too big. There's no way it's going to fit inside. It hurts!"

"Punishment hurts," I informed as I pressed a little deeper. "Focus on the discipline and know that this will happen again and again if you disobey my orders."

Her hands flailed until they found my calves and dug in.

Her breath hitched with every movement of the plug. Inch by inch, it made its passage to her depths.

"Oh, God," she mewled.

The plug was almost all the way in, spreading her hole to its limits. Her anus continued to stretch, but her pussy was clearly getting wet with desire. The tight muscles gave as she took the thickest part of the plug.

Bellamy shook her head again, her voice strained. "Emmett, I can't. It stings."

"Take a deep breath and relax. You can do this."

With a final shove that had her crying out, I pushed the plug all the way past the flared base to allow her hole to close around the much smaller stem attaching the hand-hold, locking it in place inside her.

I leaned down and placed soft kisses on her lower back, working my way to each cheek of her ass. I moved my hand beneath her weight to her clit and pinched. She pressed against my touch, silently begging me for the tender reward for her submission.

I continued to rub and stroke her bud as her body adjusted to the girth and stretch of the plug. "Now, the punishment is about to begin," I said.

"What? The plug isn't the punishment? I get it. Lesson learned. I get your message loud and clear."

I couldn't help but chuckle. "That's just the appetizer." Pressing down on her back when she tried to struggle, I said, "When I'm done with you, there will be no question in your mind to obey me when I tell you not to come. Your body will learn to obey just as your mind will." I tapped the handle of the plug for emphasis, which caused her to release a little moan.

I adjusted her body with my knee so her ass was higher up and on better display. Before she could process what would come next, I slapped her ass hard once, twice, and then a third time.

Bellamy desperately tried to wriggle loose from my grasp. "Emmett, please! I'm sorry! We don't need to do this."

I continued to spank, each swat harder than the one before. "Who's in charge, Bellamy?" I swatted her again as I asked the question.

"You are!"

"I expect my rules to be followed. I expect perfection. You knew that going into this agreement, correct?"

I brought down my palm on every inch of her firm little ass.

"Yes, I knew," she hissed as I spanked the area where her butt met her thigh. "I know what you expect. Yes!"

"You are going to learn to surrender control to me," I said as I paused the spanking and reached for the belt beside me.

I folded over the leather, knowing I'd go light on her for the first time, not truly giving her a whipping. Especially at this angle, since I couldn't exactly get a swing like I could if I had her bent over the bed. Although, it was no doubt her first time getting a belting would definitely not feel like I was going light on her.

I brought down the leather to her pinkened flesh, and she howled out. "Emmett. Stop! I said I'm sorry."

"Sorry for what?" I asked as I brought down the belt again.

She cried out, and though the spanking had intensified, she seemed to be melting into my body, no longer wiggling and fighting the punishment. Her body submitted, and I knew she wasn't just telling me what I wanted to hear or to avoid any more of a spanking.

"For not taking your rules and your orders seriously. I will from now on, Sir."

I belted her one more time and decided to give her mercy, since she addressed me the proper way without me having to ask for it. My submissive was learning fast.

The minute I stopped her spanking, I lifted her off my lap and placed her on her back on the bed. She instantly spread her legs, welcoming me to come and take her. To claim her as mine. I could see the wetness of her pussy. I could smell her arousal.

"Fuck me, Emmett," she nearly purred. "I want you."

I leaned over her, so close that my lips could touch hers, but they didn't. "I told you that you'd beg for my cock after I spank you. Beg."

"Please, Emmett. Please. I want your cock," she pleaded like the good girl she now was.

It took every last ounce of control I had left in my body as I stood up. Taking a calming breath, I said, "No sex after a punishment. Bad girls don't get to come."

She bolted up into a sitting position with wide eyes. "What? Are you kidding me?" She shifted her ass on the bed. "What about... what about the plug inside me?"

I smirked as I began to put my belt back on. "Not kidding at all. And you'll wear the plug until we go to sleep."

"Emmett!"

I shot her a warning look. "I would tread lightly right now and not push me. I can continue the punishment if you're still feeling feisty. Do you need more of my belt to go along with that plug that *will* stay in your ass?"

All the fight that had suddenly surged through her body when I told her there would be no sex dissipated as she took a deep breath and said, "No, *sir*. That won't be necessary."

I turned my back on her so she wouldn't be able to see the smile I could no longer hide. I wanted to remain firm and dominant for a little bit longer, even though my cock wanted to be buried deep inside her. I wanted to kiss her and praise her for submitting to a true punishment, but it wasn't time. She needed a firm and strong hand right now. I needed to stay focused on the goal and what I managed to do tonight. My little brat had been tamed... for now.

6

BELLAMY

My ass was sore all the next day, and I just knew it would be sore tomorrow too. I was doing a fine job of ignoring Emmett for most of the day. I slept in for as long as His Highness would allow, then it was all "Yes, Sir" *this* and "Yes, Sir" *that* until I thought I might stab him in the face with my fingernails, except I'd spent an hour this afternoon giving myself a manicure, and it would be a shame to waste it by scratching his eyes out.

That was, until he started completely ignoring me for what he called "work time." When he finally shut his laptop lid five hours later and announced, "All right, it's time for some fresh air," around five, I all but leaped off the bed. He hadn't even stopped working for lunch. Mrs. H had brought our food to us, and if I had to stay cooped up in this bedroom for another minute, I was going to go stir-crazy.

I wasn't sure if Emmett sensed my nervous energy or if he genuinely wanted to go for a walk himself, but I didn't care. I'd never considered that the one thing that might make this whole thing impossible for me was the part where I was cooped up for three months. It wasn't the staying inside part that was a problem; it was the silence. Emmett liked it absolutely silent while he worked.

When I was at home, Mom always had the TV on in the background, and I was usually watching some YouTube or TikTok or something on my phone, plus music on most of the time too.

I *hated* silence. It drove me absolutely batty.

Heaven to me was an EDM club with a bass thumping so loud you couldn't hear yourself think. Thinking was so goddamn overrated. I'd do anything to get away from my own head sometimes.

I had my shoes on by the time Emmett turned around. "Ready," I chirped cheerily.

He lifted an eyebrow but didn't say anything. He just went to the dresser and got a pair of socks. I tried not to watch him carefully pull them on. It was stupid that even his feet were sexy. I looked out the window instead. It was October, and all the leaves were in full fire colors.

I got up and went to wait impatiently by the door.

"Maybe we should stay in, to teach my little subbie some patience."

I looked over my shoulder at him, mouth open. But then he tilted his head. "You did take your punishment well last night though."

I shut my mouth, clenching my teeth so I didn't shout something at him that would earn me another punishment and have him taking away my walk. One thing was true about all he'd said—people rarely said no to me in my life before now. At least so directly.

Either way, I kept my mouth shut as he got his shoes on and led the way out of the room, through the hallway, and down the staircase. It was strange walking through the mansion while it was so quiet. The only other time I'd been out was for breakfast, and we'd just walked to a morning breakfast room that was on the second story.

But I wasn't bothering too much looking around. The air in here felt stale, and I wanted *out*. Besides, I was used to old houses and antiques. I didn't know why people had such a hard-on for old places like this.

I'd always dreamed of escaping and seeing things that were new. New places, new faces. Where no one knew a goddamned thing about your past or cared who your grandfather was or wasn't.

Finally, we pushed through the large double doors into the fresh autumn air. I paused for only a moment on the steps after Emmett shut the doors behind us and breathed in deep.

God, that was good. I hurried down the stone steps of the huge house to the gravel below. Emmett stayed beside me, but I had the feeling that he was hurrying at my unexpected burst of speed.

He'd probably think I was crazy if I broke into a run. But the fresh air against my skin felt so damn good. I was wearing leggings and a tank top, but Georgia stayed sultry and warm until well into mid-November some years, including this one.

"You got somewhere you gotta be?" Emmett asked, still easily keeping pace beside me with his long legs. I wasn't quite running, but I was putting space between us and Oleander Mansion looming behind us.

We were heading across the yard into the field beyond. I could glimpse a lake in the distance, the surface winking in the sunlight.

I just shrugged and kept heading forward. "It just feels good to get out," I said. "I don't like being crammed up in one place for too long."

He laughed. "You do realize that's part of the Trials. It's psychological as much as anything. What did you think you were signing up for?"

I glanced back at him, then forward again. I wasn't ready to get into that with him right now, if ever. My reasons for being here were my own. I still had my pride.

"Bellamy." His voice was sharp with that commanding edge. "Stop."

Huffing in annoyance, I did. And I was as annoyed at having to stop as I was at the fact that I could tell the difference in his normal conversation tone and his... well, his *Dom* tone was the only way to describe it.

I was also annoyed at the way my sex clenched just hearing it.

"What?" I crossed my arms over my chest. His eyes moved down briefly, registering the gesture. I dropped my arms, frustrated at the way he noticed every little damn thing.

"I won't demand everything at once," he said, "but you *will* give me a little bit."

I jutted my chin out. "All I promised in this bargain was to give you my body."

He smiled, and I wanted to smack it off his face. "That's where you're mistaken. Now, let's take a nice, leisurely walk around the lake instead of like a bat out of hell, and you can tell me why you still live in Darlington. When we were seniors, you were modeling and dreaming of being an Instagram influencer. I always thought you'd skip college to go flaunting around Ibiza or something like that."

Hearing him talk about the past hit a nerve. I couldn't say it didn't. And at the same time, it sounded like a completely different universe. A different person.

God, had those really been my dreams?

I shrugged and kept walking. We had slowed down as we came to the lake, walking the perimeter, but I still felt that restless energy that had me wanting to bolt.

"Bellamy?" he pushed, because of course he did. He was like a splinter that wouldn't let you forget it. "What happened?"

"I don't know," I said, waving a hand dismissively. "Life?"

"Bellamy." His tone said it all. He wouldn't drop it until I gave him more.

"Fine," I breathed, shooting him a glare but being careful not to roll my eyes. "Dad died, okay? Dad died right at the end of senior year and it—" *Brought the whole house of cards tumbling down.* "—sucked."

He nodded, his brows drawing together. "I remember hearing about that. My dad went to the funeral."

I shrugged. "Well, they were in the Order together."

His eyes cut my way. "You knew your dad was in the Order?"

"Mom told me about it after he died."

I found out a lot about my dad after he passed away. I'd never really known him when he was alive beyond him being a sort of benign absent presence in our lives. Always traveling for "business." Ha.

"Do you miss him?"

"No." I didn't bother lying or putting emotion I didn't feel into my voice.

I could feel Emmett's frown without looking. Instead, I looked out at the lake and breathed in the fresh air that blew across it, making small waves lap at the edge of the rocky beach.

"Does your mother know you're here?" he asked next. "Aren't you supposed to be marrying an Atlanta banker or something?"

I barely contained my scoff. Oh if only he knew. This was Mommy Dearest's *idea*. She still clung to all this blue-blood bullshit. Ironic, considering Emmett was new money. But if he was good enough for the Order, he was good enough for her.

Her father had been in the Order, and I knew she thought if I could just snag me a husband who was Order material, everything would be put back to rights. The nightmare of the last half decade could just *poof*, disappear!

Because Mom thought that at the end of this, Emmett would fall in love with me and propose marriage, just like the last few Initiates had to their belles.

Ha. *Hahahahahahahaha*. I could die laughing. I could just die.

Then again, she'd always been easily deluded.

She'd believed Dad's bullshit for all those years, after all.

I looked him in the eyes and told him the truth. It was in the contract we'd signed that I never lie to him. "She knows where I am."

His eyebrows went up. I'd surprised him. He didn't know it, but I was full of surprises.

I decided to turn the tables on him, done with answering questions for the time being. "Why are *you* here?" I asked, shaking my head. "I always thought you were different from the others."

His jaw stiffened. "Why? 'Cause I'm not as good as them? 'Cause my pappy's *pappy* wasn't in the Order?" he mocked.

I was *this* close to rolling my eyes but stopped myself just in time. I shook my head. "No," I said pointedly. "Because you were always the nice one who wasn't a pompous jackass. And you still are. Everyone knows about the charities you donate to instead of buying Bentleys or private jets. You don't need the Order like the others do. You're richer than God."

"Oh," he grunted, his brow scrunched like he was still looking for the trap in what I said. "Well, the way I see it, I'm here because we're all on the same playing field. If everyone's rich, no one's trying to take advantage of me or play me. Everyone has power and wealth; I'm among equals. I'll be accepted or rejected on my own merits."

Did he really think that? Didn't he know every game was rigged? The Elders had been able to afford to kick Sully out, but Emmett? With as much money and influence as he could bring to the table... did he really think the Elders would be that stupid? Of course, the degree to which they wanted him to be malleable to their control... now *that* was another matter. So maybe they *would* make Emmett and me jump through more hoops than most in these damn Trials after all.

Men drunk on power never imagined they could lose it. My father certainly hadn't, and look what that had done to us.

But if Emmett didn't like the idea of people using him or trying to take advantage of him, then he could never, ever discover why my mother had sent me here. He'd hate the thought of someone trying to manipulate him into marriage. Not that it would ever matter, but still.

"What about the belles?" I asked, putting it in the hypothetical. "Do you respect them less, because they're here to take advantage of rich men?"

He looked me in the eye. "They're honest about it, so I respect it. No one's lying to anyone here. And the difference is"—he smirked—"it's not my money they're getting. It's the Order's. So that brings us back to my original question. Why are *you* here, Bellamy Carmichael? You've got the bluest of blue blood of anyone in Darlington County."

I just smiled at him as I walked backward toward the house, daring to give him a little wink. "A woman's got to have her secrets. Race you back?" And then I took off running before he could answer.

7

EMMETT

I remembered fantasizing about asking Bellamy Carmichael to prom. I pictured how beautiful she would be on my arm with our color-matching outfits, her corsage, my boutonnière, and the excitement of youth. We would have made such a cute couple... in my head.

But no.

Girls like Bellamy Carmichael did not attend proms with boys like me.

But now, as I had the most beautiful woman in Darlington County on my arm, as I escorted her to the Oleander's All Hallow's Eve party, I got to correct history in a very dark, very kinky, and very perfect way.

But tonight, we would not be the "cute couple." Hot as fuck partners in a twisted game of wealth and power, yes. But not *cute*.

She wore a black satin dress that skimmed her upper thigh. The dress was so short that if she touched her toes, I no doubt would've been able to see the curve of her ass peeking from beneath. Her long blonde hair cascaded down her back, and although she tried to pin it up when she first got dressed, I ordered her to keep it long and free. I needed something to take hold of tonight. The black, five-inch Jimmy Choos she wore showed off her muscular legs, and I had never wanted to lick something so badly in my life. I wanted my tongue to caress every inch of her calves, her knees, her inner thigh....

I could feel her energy as she buzzed with excitement when the black dress arrived for her to wear. It wasn't just that she could get dressed for tonight's Trial, but that she actually got to attend the very coveted and secret party that everyone in Darlington knew about but didn't get invited to. It was not just for the members of the Order, but also for the most debauched fuckers who came out to play for this one open event at the mansion.

"I've always wanted to go to this," Bellamy said under her breath as we approached the ballroom. "I've heard a lot of stories."

"If you actually heard *true* stories, I'm not too sure you'd be so willing to attend."

She glanced up at me with a delicious twinkle in her eye and a smirk. "What makes you so sure of that?"

I paused right before we reached the door. I could hear the heavy bass of electronic music on the other side. There would be no fancy orchestra and champagne flutes tonight. Oh no. Not tonight. Tonight was all about connecting with the devil. It was about getting as close to wicked sins as you could get when it came to your hungry, sexual desires.

"Rules," I stated, spinning her so she had to face me directly.

Her thick eyelashes fluttered as she looked up at me and waited for what I had to say.

"I'm in charge. Me. You do as I say, and you don't question or hesitate at all. Though it's a party, the eyes of the

Elders will be on us. They'll always be watching, and what we do or do not do tonight will be noticed."

"What exactly is it we'll be doing?"

"Whatever I want," I nearly growled as I spun her back around and led us into the ballroom.

The white ballroom had morphed to black. Candlelight flickered against blood-red roses, and thick velvet curtains —the color of the night's sky—blanketed the walls. Heavy beats of the music vibrated against my body, and it only added to the sizzle of sin dripping from the thoughts of the guests attending. The party had just started, but I could already smell the sex in the room. And not just any sex. Whips, chains, leather, and every sex toy imaginable were the decor tonight. Black, raw, primal, and erotic was the dress code.

Welcome to the All Hallow's Eve party.

Some would call this a BDSM party. But there was no consent present beyond that of walking in the doors. Once you walked past these walls, all bets were off. You were at the mercy of your partner. You were his, just as he was yours. The rules of what was right and wrong blended. *Yes* or *no* morphed into a new saying. A saying so powerful that it could only be whispered behind closed doors tonight. At this party. On All Hallow's Eve.

Fuck me hard, harder, harder....

There was no soft in this room.

It was too loud to hear Bellamy's breathing, but the enhanced rise and fall of her shoulders and chest told me all I needed to know. She was nervous. And good... she should've been.

I scanned the room to see where the Elders were and noticed that they were already watching us enter. Just as I told Bellamy—tonight's Trial had begun.

I lowered my mouth to her ear and said, "Let's begin."

Her wide eyes turned up to me. "Don't we at least get a drink first?"

I didn't answer but instead pulled her over to a hand-crafted St. Andrew's cross that mastered the room. There were so many tools of the trade scattered around the ballroom ranging from spanking benches, tables with leather straps, cages, and chaises meant to be fucked on. But the cross remained open, and it would be a real shame for it not to be utilized for the night. It truly stood in the middle of the room in all its glory, and it was time for Bellamy and me to take center stage.

Though Bellamy walked beside me, I could feel her pace slow as we approached. It required me to tug her slightly as her feet seemed to drag.

"Are you afraid?" I asked as I assisted her up the single step to get on the platform of the cross.

"No," she lied. Yes, it was quite obvious she lied.

"You should be."

I didn't waste any time as I pressed her face-first against the wood, kissing her briefly on her shoulder and then the back of her head as I did. I took her wrist in my hand and extended her arm up high, where leather cuffs were waiting. When I secured the leather around her tiny wrist, I followed it with a kiss.

Yes, I could be gentle... when I wanted to be.

I repeated the exact action on her other wrist as well as each ankle, spreading her wide. She truly became an X of beauty. She wasn't naked... yet. But that was because I had a plan. I always had a plan.

I leaned into her ear and whispered, "You wait right here. I'll be back."

I watched her snap her head to look at me, her body

trying to pull her breasts away from the wood to no avail. "Wait! What? You can't just leave me here all by myself! I'm tied up and can't move. You can't—"

"I can," I said, as I turned toward a bar serving cocktails.

I was pretty sure any Initiate would be intimidated knowing the Elders were watching, but I really wasn't. I'd been watched and scrutinized my entire life. I was used to always being on display of sorts and having to prove my worth. Tonight would be no different.

But the Elders could wait for me to at least get a whiskey down my throat.

When I made my way back to Bellamy with drink in hand, I couldn't help but find amusement in the way her ass looked squirming against her binds. She should've been smarter than that. Did she really think I'd give her the ability to escape?

"You're going to rub your wrists and ankles raw with all that movement," I chastised as I approached the cross.

"You asshole. You just left me here. I can't see anything and don't know what's—"

I placed the whiskey at her lips. "Drink," I interrupted. "You said you wanted a drink first."

She had no choice but to swallow the brown liquid, and I loved that she was muzzled for now. I took mental note just how much the thought of gagging her made my dick twitch and would be sure to do that act later.

Knowing the Elders would be growing impatient, I pulled the whiskey glass from her lips and finished off the remainder of the drink myself. I then walked over to a nearby table where a leather flogger, among other toys, was on display for use. Bellamy was able to turn her head far enough to see exactly where I was going and what I was picking up. I glanced up at her as I felt the weight of the flogger in my hand and raised an eyebrow at her. Her eyes widened, she licked her lips, and she turned her face back to the wood as if preparing herself for what was to come.

Noticing she was still wearing her black dress, I instantly knew this couldn't be. Though she was extremely sexy in what she wore, I needed to show off just how beautiful a woman she was. That... and I wanted to see the marks as I whipped her. Reaching for an intricately jeweled dagger, I paused for a moment as wicked thoughts ran through my head of all the acts I could do with the blade.

I marched over with my tools, brought the knife to the fabric of her dress, and began slicing it off her. The metal cut through the satin easily, and the dress cascaded to her heeled feet in a pool of darkness. She inhaled deeply as I cut the dress off her but didn't say a single word.

My cock grew hard at the sight but more at the knowledge that the Elders were watching.

Watch, fuckers. Watch the most beautiful woman in this room cry out my name and beg for my dick by the time I'm done with her. Watch.

Once she was naked, I placed the knife down at my feet and picked up the flogger. *Let's begin.*

I slapped the leather against her ass first, not hard but as a warning of what was to come. I wanted her to get used to the feel of leather kissing her bare flesh. She gasped as I did so, flinched slightly, but didn't turn her head to face me.

Funny girl. Ignoring me wouldn't make me go away.

I brought the flogger down again, harder this time, and smirked when she cried out in surprise. Not pausing, I repeated the step a few more times, not stopping the flogging until her entire ass was pink and swollen. Her whimpers and mewls blended with the sound of the music as I did so, and I had never heard such a sensual song in my life.

The harmony of her cries and the beats of the techno only made me want to add to the melody.

Still holding the flogger by my side, I approached her ear and whispered, "Does it fucking hurt?"

Her eyes were closed, and her lips parted, with heavy breaths escaping. "Nothing I can't handle."

I chuckled. "It's not like you have much choice in the matter, but I do appreciate your bravado."

All around us were cries of pleasure and pain and sex a plenty. Flogging Bellamy was no different or more special than what the other men in the room were doing with their partners, so I knew I needed to up my game.

Dropping the flogger, I reached for the knife and took notice of how the handle was ribbed with rubies, sapphires, and emeralds. Phallic in nature, so it made complete sense what my next step would be. I took a minute to first bring the blade to Bellamy's cheek and rest it flat against her face. I wanted her to know exactly what it was I was using as our delicious little toy.

Her lip trembled as she said, "You aren't going to cut me, are you? Please don't hurt me."

I applied pressure to the knife. "I would never cut perfection. But I can't promise not to hurt you. I love the sound of your cries."

Flipping the dagger around so that I carefully held where the base met the blade, I brought the jeweled handle to her pussy and caressed the intricate ridges along her folds. Unsatisfied not seeing it all happen up close, I decided to kneel, looking up between her spread legs. The slickened flesh of her cunt greeted me as I did so.

"I'm going to fuck you with this," I informed.

Her body tensed, but a moan released the minute I thrust the handle into her tight little hole.

I had the best view in the room, but I could feel the eyes of the Elders burning a hole in the back of my damn head.

Good. Watch, assholes.

This is what real power looks like.

There wasn't a woman in this room who was as hungry for a cock in this moment as my girl. I could see it. I could smell it. And as I swiped my finger along her pussy, I could feel it. Bringing my finger to my lips... I could taste it.

Bellamy's pussy swallowed the gems as I pumped the knife in and out of her. Juices coated the handle, and there was no doubt in my mind that she wanted more. Her moans became louder than the music, and I noticed the muscles in her legs tighten and quiver.

My little pain slut was going to come on this blade for all to see.

I continued to jam it in and out of her, harder and deeper with each pass. I could tell she was close, so close that the minute I reached with my free hand to her clit and pinched, a scream cut through the air as her cream leaked on my fingers.

Pulling out the knife, I tossed it to the ground and kissed my way up her leg, her ass, her back, and then up to her ear, where I whispered, "Such a good girl you are. There will be a reward."

8

BELLAMY

He had to carry me back up to the room. I maybe could have walked up the stairs, but he swept me up in his arms the moment he finished releasing me from the St. Andrew's Cross, and I went limp the moment he did.

No one had ever... I mean, obviously no one had ever done anything like that to me. I couldn't.... My brain still felt fuzzy, even as my body buzzed with the insane body-shaking orgasm that blasted me while he fucked me with the jeweled hilt of his blade, the entire room watching on.

I didn't feel like myself. Was it possible to orgasm so hard that you left your own damn body? Because that was what it felt like right now, like I was still hovering outside my skin even as I clung to Emmett's neck. I wasn't sure I was quite ready to come back to reality yet either.

And when we got to our room and Emmett laid me down in the center of the lush comforter, all I could do was stare up at him.

"What?" He smirked. "No witty repartee about me putting you on display like that and showing them exactly how hungry your cunt is for anything your master has to feed it?"

My legs spasmed and my mouth dropped open, but I didn't say a word. He grinned as he towered over me, and it was the grin of a shark. He ripped his suit jacket off and was just as vicious as he attacked the buttons on his dress shirt, finally giving up and tugging it along with his undershirt off over his head.

Then he fell onto the bed, crawling between my legs with his huge, powerful shoulders rippling. I gasped as he grabbed my thighs and pried my legs open wide.

"You did so well tonight," he breathed out right over my pussy, and I writhed underneath him, blinking and trying to orient myself. "God, you're beautiful."

I still felt floaty, and this didn't seem quite real—him showering me with compliments. Every time he did, the glow in my pussy pulsed. He'd been so rough with me downstairs, but now he laid the gentlest kisses up my inner thigh. First, my left thigh, then my right. But each time he got to my center, he pulled back and moved back down my leg.

I blinked in confusion, and my hips moved restlessly. I felt drunk with the buzzing pleasure. What the hell had he done to me downstairs? But I didn't want to come to the surface yet, so I didn't fight when he held my hips firmly in place as he continued his torturous advance and retreat.

His lips were impossibly soft, and then—oh God, his *tongue*.

I whimpered when he licked along the crease between my leg and my sex and yet again pulled away.

"Please," I moaned, my fingers clenching the comforter.

His head lifted. "Please, *what*?" Seeing him there, muscled as a Greek god, positioned between my legs, my body convulsed, but it wasn't enough to come, even though I was on a razor's edge.

There was only one thing to say, and in that moment, it was more than just a game we were playing or something I'd agreed to for a few moments, something that should have terrified me but didn't. "Please, Master," I whispered, near tears from my need.

His eyes flared, and for a moment, he just held me there, our gazes locked.

And then slowly, ever so deliberately, he lowered his head and licked up the center of me. I was undone. I couldn't hold his gaze anymore; I was barely tethered to this universe.

I screamed as my head flew back.

I pulsed and juiced into his mouth as he suckled and licked me clean. And then I came even harder, my hips grinding against his face. He grasped my ass in a rough grip, eating me out roughly now, and that was even more—

Oh... Oh God.

I screamed as I came so hard.

And then he was crawling up the bed, shucking his pants in the same motion. My legs opened to him, and then in one stroke, he filled me.

And filled me *deep*.

The headboard cracked against the wall as he grasped the hair at the nape of my neck with one hand and kissed me deep.

We'd had sex before, obviously, but it had never been like this. I tried to wrap my arms around him, but he grasped my wrists and pinned me to the bed as he fucked me, dominating me to the very end.

And the orgasm that began with his gentle, seeking tongue started right back up again as his surging cock slid in and out of me. At first, it was just the outer friction, but then he shifted and lit up that inner part.

I gasped my cries into his mouth, and he pulled back. "Eyes," he demanded. "Scream my name as you come. Let the whole mansion know who your master is."

His dominant commands made me soar higher, and I screamed, "Emmett," as I clenched around his cock and came and came, and then I rode it higher and longer.

And he kept fucking me and owning my body in ways I'd never even suspected were possible.

I'd just finally finished the orgasm when he demanded, "Again. I'm coming now."

And I felt it in his posture, the way his glistening muscles were clenching, and how his jaw went tight. He was about to come, and it was—

I was set off again, me, who'd never been multi-orgasmic before this man. "Emmett," I gasped in a hoarse, high-pitched whine as an orgasm lit from my belly to the top of my scalp and then landed back in my pussy.

He shoved deep, slamming my wrists into the mattress and pinning me with his gaze, and his jaw tensed so hard as the vein in his forehead pulsed. And I felt the flood of him inside me as he came.

Our gazes locked, both of us connected in ecstasy, him mastering me, and I was lost, so lost to him and to pleasure and a million other things I didn't understand but didn't have to. I gave in, my mind blank as pleasure tsunami'd through my body from top to bottom.

I only went limp when he did, both of us collapsing simultaneously. He slid slightly to the side so his weight wasn't crushing me, but he was still on top of me. The solid warmth and pressure of him—it was the safest and most complete I'd ever felt. If I'd been in my right mind, maybe it would have scared me. But I wasn't in any mind. I was in the beautiful blankness where he'd taken me. I had no responsibilities but to trust him here.

When he started to roll away from me, I thought I might cry, but he came right back. He had a soft, warm wet cloth.

And he held me in his arms as he washed me. I was silent, pliant as a doll, watching everything he did with big, wide eyes. But he was far from quiet.

"You're so fucking beautiful," he murmured as he slid the warm cloth between my legs. "Precious."

He rolled me over, and with hands so gentle I could barely believe they belonged to Emmett, he rubbed some sort of herbal-smelling salve into the places where he flogged me earlier in the night. Almost instantly, I became groggy.

And the more he whispered about how proud he was of me for how well I'd done, the warmer and sleepier I got. No one had ever....

My eyes were wet, and I shut them so I wouldn't cry.

As I came slowly back into my body, his hands still soothing my sore places, my thoughts were a jumble. No one had ever expected so much of me, and I'd never tried as hard as I had tonight. I'd tried to be perfect tonight, and it hadn't been easy. I'd been terrified of what was going to happen when he first started securing me to that damn cross. But he'd been beside me, and that made it possible.

Letting him nurture me like this... it made me feel even more naked than when I'd been down there in front of all the Elders, but I didn't pull away. Still though, I couldn't look at him, especially after the sex we'd just had. It felt like he looked straight into me at the end there, and I didn't know....

He was seeing more of me than anyone else in the world ever had. What was I supposed to do with any of this?

"Shhh," he murmured like he could hear my turbulent thoughts. He climbed in the bed behind me. His knees notched behind mine, and his chest cemented to the curve of my back. When his arm came around my waist, my entire body relaxed back against him, and my churning thoughts quieted until the surface of my mind became as smooth as a placid lake in the silence of a still morning.

"Sleep," he commanded, and like every other one of his orders that night, my body almost instantly obeyed.

9

EMMETT

Though the weather was cooling down in Georgia, the heat of the day was still stifling in the confines of the Oleander. We spent entirely too many days cooped up inside, waiting for our next Trial, and it was starting to get to me. And based on how irritable Bellamy was getting at times, I could tell the same could be said for her. No one warned me just how hard the months in the Oleander would be. The Trials were nothing in comparison to just having idle time on our hands.

"Today seems like the perfect day for swimming," I announced as I closed my laptop and stood with a stretch.

Bellamy looked up from the book she was reading and shook her head. "I didn't bring a bathing suit."

I reached for the book and pulled it out of her hands. "You don't need one."

Not giving her a chance to argue any longer, I took her by the hand and led her out of our room, out of the mansion, and toward the lake.

It had been quite some time since we'd first been to the lake, and the minute I saw it as we approached, I regretted that we hadn't come more often. Water lapped against the shoreline, the reflection of the sun causing bands of color and light to dance across the surface.

Toeing off my shoes, I turned to face Bellamy. "Let's get in. The water's going to feel great."

It was a bit chillier than I expected, and yet, after an initial quick intake of breath, I lifted my arms and dove beneath the surface. I swam underwater until I needed to breathe, surfacing and shoving my hair out of my face. Treading water, I looked toward the shore and was surprised to see Bellamy just standing there watching.

"Are you coming in?" I called out.

"I'm fine." She looked at a nearby boulder on the shoreline and made her way over there to sit on it.

"It's hot out. Come on." I swam back toward the shore so I could convince her to test the waters. "It's not too cold. Promise."

She shook her head. "It's not that. It's just—"

I watched her kick off her sandals and put her toes in the water. "I don't have my bathing suit on."

"Nor do I," I pointed out. "I think we're past the bashful stage." I lifted my arms out of the water to motion around me. "And it's just you and me out here. You don't have to worry about anyone seeing you."

Her eyes went to the water, and I could see she was considering it.

"Come on," I prodded. "Do I have to come get you and carry you in?"

She laughed. "No. I can do it myself." She stood and pointed at me. "But don't get my hair wet."

It took everything in me not to roll my eyes. Southern girls and their hair....

But I became quickly distracted when she began to undress. My cock hardened the moment she hooked her fingers into the waistband of her shorts and pulled them over her shapely ass. As she pulled her tank top over her head, she gave me a wicked smile. Unclipping her bra and dropping it on the ground, she stepped out of her panties and stood as I scanned her entire nude body from head to toe in the light of the sun.

This was different than at a Trial or in the privacy of our bedroom. She was exposed, vulnerable, and more seductive than ever before.

"I'm not really a swimmer," she confessed, not giving me a chance to respond as she stepped past me and entered the water.

She lowered her body but was extra careful to stop at her neck, not letting her hair or face get wet.

"You know," I began, "it's okay to mess up your perfect makeup and your blown-out hair. I swear I won't tell anyone that you actually went swimming."

It dawned on me that she never let me see her without a full face of makeup and her hair perfectly styled. She wouldn't leave even the bathroom after a shower until she was completely put together. This wasn't unusual from dating women in Georgia. It was like they were groomed to always have lipstick ready and a blow dryer in hand.

"My mother would have a stroke, knowing I was doing this much in the lake. Ladies don't skinny dip, and we most certainly don't do it in broad daylight," she said, her southern accent strong as she spoke.

"Don't you ever want to break the perfect southern rules once in a while?" I asked, following her deeper into the water.

"All the time," she answered. "But it's best you see the

good side of me. No one needs to see me without makeup. It's not a pretty sight."

Though she had a smile on as she said the words and seemed as if she was joking, I found sadness in the words.

"I disagree," I replied, taking hold of her arm and stopping her from her swim, with her head bobbing out of the water. "I don't think you need all that makeup to be pretty. You're naturally beautiful."

She huffed. "I was taught at a very young age that natural beauty does not exist without assistance. I think I've worn lipstick since I was ten, when my mother told me I was cursed with thin lips."

We both stood in the water, looking at each other. She was smiling, but I wasn't.

"That's a shame, Bellamy. Your mother should have never made you feel like you aren't perfect in every way."

"No one's perfect." She darted her eyes away from me as she said the words. "But that's what smoke and mirrors are for. We can make anyone pretty with enough blush and eyeshadow."

I took a step closer to her and said, "Dive under the water with me."

Her eyes widened. "Have you not heard a word I said? I'm not going to mess up—"

"I've heard every single thing you've said, and I want to prove you wrong. Dive under the water with me."

"No."

"Don't make me dunk you."

"You better not."

"Or what?" I teased.

"Emmett!" she squealed when I took hold of her tightly.

"I'm not going to force you. But come on, Bellamy. Let loose. Stop letting your mother stand here in the lake with us. Break the rules for once in your life. Stop listening to your mom. Come swim with me."

I could actually see her considering my words, and then finally, without warning, she dove into the water—hair and all.

I hooted in excitement as I too dove in and swam with her deeper, untethered by the rules of an old-fashioned society.

After several moments, we both emerged from the water, breathless and feeling more alive than we both had since arriving at the Oleander. Freedom.

Her wet hair clung to her face, her makeup mostly gone other than a few smears of black around her eyes.

"I've never seen anyone prettier than you right now," I complimented, and I meant every word.

I captured Bellamy's mouth with mine, demanding more of her taste with every caress of my tongue. I couldn't get enough of this woman. She was like a fucking drug, and she already had me addicted. I didn't think it was possible for her to get any more beautiful than I already found her, but with the water streaming down her perfect skin and her hair hanging wildly around her face, I didn't want to ever see her any other way.

I wanted to be inside her, a hunger I could barely control. And then again after that. There weren't enough hours in the day for how much I wanted to continue fucking her. Claiming her. Making her mine. The primal side took over, but there was something more...

Something deep inside that scared me if I thought too much about it.

Bellamy broke away from the kiss and stared up at me with her big blue eyes. "I must look like a mess right now."

"You're beautiful. So much more beautiful than words

can describe. It's such a shame that your mother and our society have made you doubt that. You don't need fakeness to be gorgeous, because you are, all on your own."

She pressed her naked body against mine, and I became completely undone. Any control I had vanished the minute her thighs touched mine.

I spun her around and pressed my chest against her back. I cupped her breasts with each of my hands and nestled my hard cock against the seam of her ass. Nibbling her ear, I whispered, "You do something to me. You bring out this animal need inside to claim you as mine."

As I nibbled on the column of her throat, the memory of the Trials and all our sex flashed before me, but something felt different this time.

I didn't have to fuck her.

And she didn't have to let me.

"You make me feel... different. Free to be me," she said as she tilted her head more to the side, giving me better access to bite at and kiss on her neck. Her tiny whimper of lust had my cock twitching.

"Never feel you have to be fake again," I told her between my kissing assault upon her neck, her shoulder, and her collarbone.

As I massaged her breasts between my fingers, my cock throbbed even harder when Bellamy moaned in pleasure, clearly not feeling she had to hide her growing desire.

"I don't want you to stop," she purred while reaching behind her, grabbing hold of my ass, and pulling me even closer to her. The act caused my cock to slide deeper within the cheeks of her ass, so deliciously close to her tight, forbidden hole.

"I had no intention of stopping."

Lowering my hand away from teasing one of her nipples,

I ran my fingertips down her stomach to her mound, cupping it while I nearly growled into her ear. Finding her clit, I pressed lightly and moved my finger in a gentle circular motion. I loved hearing the catch in her breath and thrived on how it was obvious she enjoyed my touch and even wanted more when she gyrated against my hand. I knew I could make her come this way, but I wanted to keep her on the edge for my ultimate goal.

Taking hold of my cock with my other hand, I guided my hardness past the folds of her pussy and thrust inside her silky warmth. Moaning loudly, I began pushing and pulling, feeling the walls of her sex squeeze tightly around me. The water of the lake flowed between our bodies as the small waves caused by our motion licked our flesh.

Bellamy clung to my hand that still rested on her pussy, joining my moans with her own. "Emmett," she said repeatedly between her gasps. The sound of pleasure leaving her lips captivated me completely.

Still with another goal in mind, I pulled out of her tight pussy, took hold of my cock again, but this time guided it to her puckered back entrance.

I had to have her there.

I wanted to claim her in the most intimate and yet primal of ways.

Being the perfect submissive—even if she didn't know it yet—Bellamy bent over ever so slightly, aiding in my pursuit. She pressed against the tip of my cock when it reached the tiny hole. Her simple action silently told me she wanted me inside her ass just as much as I did.

She gave a sharp gasp as the tip of my dick broke the surface of her anus, and all I had to do was push. Very slowly, I stretched her, paying close attention to her mewling and whimpers for any sign of real distress or serious pain. But all I got were sounds of lust and animal-istic passion.

Wrapping her wet hair in my fist, I gave it a tug until she turned to look back at me. "Relax," I coached. "Allow me to enter."

Her eyes were glazed, her mouth slightly open as she nodded her understanding, and I could actually feel the walls of her hole loosen to accept my size. It was all I needed to push farther.

My cock twitched when she moaned loudly, not caring if anyone at a distance could hear. She unleashed her darkest desires even under the brightest sunlight. Rewarding her, I moved my finger, which still rested on her clit, hoping I could make her come with my cock rooted deep inside her ass.

"I'm going to go deeper, harder," I warned.

She nodded and groaned loudly. "Your finger. Your cock inside me. All of it—" She gasped when I pushed even deeper. "—is going to make me come again."

"Yes, beautiful. Come while my dick is in your ass. Come for me, Bellamy."

I wasn't going to last much longer but waited until I could hear her repeated moans of absolute passion become cries of completion. The spasms of the walls of her ass around my cock were all it took for me to unleash inside her. Electric jolts of pleasure ran through every vein in my body.

It took Bellamy turning around and kissing me gently on the mouth to snap me out of a near out-of-body experience. Every inch of my skin buzzed with euphoria. Pulling her against my chest, I bent and kissed her forehead, her nose, her cheeks, and then her lips.

Feeling her shudder, I realized that I could feel goose bumps on her skin as I caressed her back. "You're cold."

"The lake water is cold," she said, snuggling a bit closer.

Pulling her by the hand toward the shore, I wanted to make sure she was comfortable and warm. The need to protect her and always keep her safe was like a punch to the gut. She was mine. Mine to possess but also to care for.

These feelings were foreign, but that didn't mean they didn't exist.

I couldn't deny them any longer.

Something was happening with Bellamy. Something far more than just sex in the Trials.

10

BELLAMY

Weeks passed, but ever since the lake... things had been different. Emmett still loved to master me, but it was like... I didn't even know how to explain it really. It was sweeter between us. The sex wasn't any gentler. God, if anything, ever since he'd taken my ass, he loved pushing me further and harder. But it was different, thrilling every time he took me to the edge and then cared for me afterward—both during the Trials and when it was just the two of us in the room.

I wasn't sure what to make of any of it.

But we were succeeding at the Trials, and the time was passing.

And for the first time in a long time, I was... happy. Which was absolutely insane, considering some of the things they were asking of us. The other day, I'd spent hours while men lined up and did Jell-O shots off my body. No one besides Emmett was allowed to fuck me, but I could feel his tension as other men licked and fondled me as they took their shots.

When we'd gotten back up to the room, he'd marched

me straight to the shower. There, he thoroughly scrubbed me down with a loofah and then spent the next three hours fucking me with a cock-ring on so he'd stay hard the whole time. As if to fuck the memory of anyone else's hands on me except his out of my mind.

It had definitely worked. Too well, I sometimes thought. Because thoughts of Emmett consumed me *all* the time.

I should have gotten tired of the man, being shut up with him twenty-four seven. But he thought up inventive ways of exerting his mastery when he sensed me getting restless. Sometimes, it was having me crouched at his feet while I read a book, and he'd sift his fingers through my hair. It should have felt demeaning, like he was petting a dog. But it didn't. Because I started craving his touch, and he was attuned to me.

There were days he'd order me to pleasure myself while he worked—on and off for hours. He was relentless, and I never knew what kind of mood he'd be in. But every day, usually more than once, he'd take a break and come play with me, though he called it *training* me.

The man was absolutely fascinated with my ass. Spanking it. Sticking plugs up it. Anal beads were also a particular favorite of his. And last but not least, fucking me there. He only did it once or twice a week though, like he saved it as a special treat for himself. In the meantime, he fucked me everywhere else.

He loved taking calls while he had me on my knees under his desk, fucking my face vigorously while keeping his voice monotone and businesslike. He was always fierce with his lovemaking after these calls, and I got it. Yes, he wanted to impress the Elders, but this place was designed for a kinky fuck like him.

He might not like the uncertainty of the Trials, but he

loved fucking me and dominating me in front of other men. His latest favorite trick was orgasm denial on Trial days. He'd spend hours working me up, bringing me to the brink but not letting me go over. Because he wanted the most spectacular show for the Elders. It was cruel. It drove me insane. And I dripped for his touch and with need for him unlike I'd even known I could need.

And the things he was training my body to crave... *Jesus*. Tonight was a Trial night, and all throughout the extended lunch today, he'd teased and teased and then pulled back every time my orgasm began to crest. And then when he'd gone back to work, he'd left me with a vibrator up my pussy, which he'd turn on at varying pulsing speeds all afternoon. So just when I was starting to calm down, he'd turn the damn thing on and have me at the edge again. Endless fucking torture.

At least he'd let me shower alone. I was tempted to rub one out while I was in there, but I knew better. Knowing Emmett, it was probably a test. I couldn't lie for shit to the man anymore, and he'd inevitably ask.

I knew being a *good girl* meant I'd get to come over and over tonight in front of the Elders, but disobeying meant a punishment that would last far beyond the Trial day. The last time I'd disobeyed, he'd cut me off for days. Not just no sex but giving me the silent treatment and not speaking to me either.

And it was shocking how much my newly sex-starved body rebelled after the near-constant orgasms. I'd been needy and all but begged him to give me my punishment, promising that I'd be a good girl from then on. It was just a part I was playing, I told myself. Just while we were here and I was so bored.

Yet I'd been beyond desperate when he still held off

another entire day before giving me an extended spanking that made my ass so sore I could barely sit the next day. But he'd massaged me afterward and hand-fed me the next day, making me feel so damn cared for and precious that I knew I'd undergo any humiliation to avoid that again.

I came out of the shower and smiled at him, still a little shocked at the warmth that flooded my chest every time I looked at him. It was such a new and foreign sensation.

His dark eyes came my way. I waited for his usual smile to light his face and for the secret look of heat to pass between us. I was only wearing my towel, and yes, I *might* have been trying to tempt him to break his own rules and fuck me before the Trial.

But he frowned and looked at his watch. "Why aren't you ready? We need to leave soon."

I blinked, suddenly unsure. My hands grasped the top of the towel I tied around myself. "It's no big deal. There was nothing in the box but the heels anyway, and those don't take long to put on."

He just stared at me. "But aren't you going to do something with your hair. And your—" He gestured toward me. "—makeup and all that."

My open and trusting heart crumpled and sank through the floor. I swallowed and nodded, backing up and running into the bathroom door.

He stood up, and I saw he already had his dark suit pants and white shirt on, pressed to perfection, and his gold and diamond cufflinks in. "It's just... you know we need to be perfect. The red lipstick would be good."

Away. I needed to get away from him. I turned around and fled back into the bathroom, shutting it behind me. Shutting him out. And his words.

My eyes squeezed shut, other words ringing through my

ears. My mother's words. *Never even go to the mailbox without your face on. You have to be perfect. The world is* always *watching.*

I opened my eyes and looked at myself in the mirror. My face was pale, and there were circles under my eyes. Plus, my nonexistent lips.

Emmett was such a goddamned liar. He was just like the rest of them. He didn't think I was perfect just as I was. Because I wasn't. God, wasn't that the whole point of him *mastering* me? I wasn't good enough as I was.

I'd been deluding myself to think he respected me or thought I was beautiful. And God, I'd been waltzing around the room without my makeup the last couple of weeks. Ha, I guess that showed him just how wrong he'd been about the whole makeup thing. Come to think of it, he'd been fucking me from behind a lot. Could he not even stand to look at my real face while he got off?

I yanked open the drawer with all my makeup in it and glared down at all the tools I'd used my entire life to paint myself into the perfect ideal of female desirability. I started with lip liner, drawing the line outside my actual lips to make them appear almost twice as big.

When I finally emerged, fully made up, buffed, and polished half an hour later, Emmett was standing in his full suit and tie, looking anxious.

"Cutting it close, don't you think?" he barked. "We're almost late. What kind of impression do you think that would make on the Elders?"

I wanted to bare my teeth at him and tell him to fuck off, that I didn't give a shit what a bunch of stupid, flabby old men thought.

Instead, I did what I'd done my whole life. I was a good little Southern girl. I swallowed it all down, went and put on some death-defying sparkly heels, and took his arm. He didn't waste any time sweeping us from the room. He was single-minded, after all. I was just arm candy. Meant to look beautiful and be a hot hole to fuck.

So glad he reminded me of my place before I completely lost my head, thinking this was something that it wasn't.

Usually, I felt a fizzle of excitement when we were approaching a Trial. Usually, I was excited to put on a show in front of the Elders, to enjoy that special connection between Emmett and me while we performed whatever perverted acrobatics they prepared for the evening.

But all I wanted to do right then was turn around, run back up the stairs, and scrub what felt like a pound of makeup off my face. Instead, I stepped off the last stair of the grand staircase and followed Emmett into the white ballroom—except unlike usual, there wasn't music or other naked women draping themselves over the silver-robed members.

The Elders still had on their silver robes, along with all the other members, who stood around solemnly. But there was one mahogany chair set up and, a few feet away from it, what looked like a long massage table. And that was it. The nervous pit at the center of my stomach grew as Emmett led me forward.

"Climb up, on your back," an Elder instructed me once we got to the massage table. Emmett let go of my hand, and I felt all alone as I did as I was told. I didn't like it though. I knew the Trials were supposed to get more intense as we went along, and I wasn't liking the feel of any of this. At all.

Still, I tried to keep my cool as Emmett sat down in the mahogany chair across from me.

It wasn't until a tattooed guy came out with a stool and a

box of instruments he started setting up—including a tattoo gun—that I really started freaking out.

I sat up and shook my head.

"Lie back down," Emmett ordered low, his eyes shooting daggers at me.

I lifted my hands up, my head still shaking back and forth involuntarily. "Uh uh. I don't do needles."

Emmett stood, and I could see how pissed he was. He strode over to me and pressed his hand on the center of my sternum as if to push me back down, but I smacked his hand away from me. I didn't miss the murmur that started among the Elders, but Emmett wasn't the only one who could get pissed.

"Don't touch me," I hissed.

Emmett's eyes were usually dark, but they went pitch-black at my refusal. He leaned down, and his voice was ice-cold. "You're fucking embarrassing me."

"Oh, God forbid," I scoffed under my breath.

His hand came up, and he grabbed me under my chin, forcing my face up to his. "I don't know where this bratty behavior is coming from, but you'll stop it right this second. You'll take this tattoo without another fucking word, and you'll thank them for it afterward."

I wanted to claw his eyes out. Where had the gentle man gone who wanted to protect me—and hurt me, yes, but only in ways that brought me pleasure? He was gone, and in his place was this sadistic bastard who only cared about what it looked like to the people watching on.

Put on a good show, no matter what you actually feel. Bury it all deep down. Who cared if you inside was rotten to its core? On the outside, we'd look beautiful, like we had it all together.

We'd be *perfect.*

"I fucking hate you."

He pulled back as if stung, which was just goddamned rich. I shook my head, shut my eyes, and lay down like the good little dolly all of them were paying for.

I'd get through this—somehow. I hated needles. I actually hated physical pain. The fact that Emmett made me like any of the things he did to me was testament to the spell I'd let him weave over me.

Well, that was all over and done with. Right now, tonight, with the first buzz and prick of the needle into the sensitive skin of my hip. I tensed, and my body jerked as the needle pressed against my hipbone. I struggled not to cry out. Jesus *fuck*, that hurt.

But did I think them literally tattooing their goddamned price tag on me would feel any other way? I kept my eyes shut even as tears leaked down my cheeks. The only satisfaction I took was in hoping my perfect mascara bled black.

11

EMMETT

"There's consequences for your behavior tonight," I said between clenched teeth. It was taking everything in me to keep my composure.

"Fuck you and your consequences." Bellamy stormed into our room and kicked off her shoes. "And I'm sick of your kinky dictates. Telling me where to kneel, when to suck, when to come. Enough."

"Bellamy—" I hoped she picked up the warning in my voice, because I was dangerously close to snapping and saying or doing something I'd regret.

She simply glared at me instead. "I can't believe you allowed tonight to happen!" She looked down at her hip. "I have a tattoo on my skin forever! Forever!"

"It was a Trial, Bellamy," I said, feeling rage build inside me, even though I was inhaling and exhaling slowly in search of my inner peace. "And you embarrassed us both."

She turned away from me and huffed. "Embarrassed? Are you kidding me? You're worried about how we appeared rather than—" She examined her tattoo again. "—the fact that we are marked for life! I don't know why you're acting like *your* behavior tonight is acceptable."

"What did you expect?" I asked as I walked over to the dresser that held a bottle of scotch and some crystal glasses. I needed a drink more than I ever had in my life right now. "Should I have babied you and stroked your delicate little hand while you went through a Trial that you wanted to be part of? Should I have called you 'sweetie' and treated you like a princess like you've spent your entire life?"

"You're an ass!" She pulled out some clothing from a dresser and then stormed into the bathroom, slamming the door behind herself. "You could have at least acted like a half-decent human being tonight," she called from the other side of the door.

"If you thought the Trials were going to be easy, then you were wrong. I didn't make you come to The Oleander. I didn't force you to agree to any of this," I shouted back at the door, pissed that I wasn't facing her head-on. "And I'm not going to fight with you through a fucking door!"

I walked over to a chair by the fireplace with scotch in hand and decided to ignore her for the rest of the night. We weren't going to get anywhere while we were both heated, and although this went against everything I believed in for a Dominant-and-submissive relationship, I needed to let it be for tonight.

She eventually came out of the bathroom, wearing leggings and a tank top. The simplicity in her appearance reminded me of just how beautiful she was without all the special effects makeup and attire.

Not that I was going to tell her that right now.

"And for the record," she stated in a much calmer tone, the trip to the bathroom giving us both the timeout we needed to stop the rage, "I never expected the Trials to be easy. But I did expect to have a partner in this. I expected to have someone to lean on and have support through it all. What happened tonight was just... abusive."

Her accusation was like a slap to the face. I had never been accused of being abusive in my entire life. "Abusive? Are you kidding me? How was I abusive?"

"You forced me to get the tattoo."

"The Order of the Silver Ghost forced it. The Trial forced it. Hell... our entire fucked-up situation forced it. I simply expected you to follow through with a commitment you made. If we agree to do something, then I damn well expect us to do it with perfection."

She folded down the comforter on the bed and flopped on her side. "Yes, I know, Emmett. But your perfectionist self and your sick need to please the Elders and be thought of as the best is exhausting. Why the fuck do you care so much? Who cares if we didn't perform like perfect little monkeys tonight? I sure as hell don't."

"I don't like your language, and I definitely don't like what you're saying. And didn't your mother teach you how to speak like a lady?"

My words seemed to slap her in the face just the same as her accusation of me being abusive did to me.

She was silent for several moments, and I took the time to drink my scotch and try to calm down. I didn't like how out of control I was being, but the woman had the ability to fire me up.

"I thought you were different from the rest of them," she said softly. "But you are just as much an asshole as everyone else in Darlington. Image is everything to you. You're part of the sickness that plagues this place. What you aren't willing to face is that you will never fit in here. Never. You are new money, while they are old. You try so hard, and they only laugh behind your back. The life you're trying to live is fake. Everything is fake."

"That's rich coming from you. You are the queen of fake. I had hoped you were different too, Bellamy. But you are just a prissy Southern belle who gets mad when she doesn't have men eating out of her hand and putting her on pedestals."

Tears welled up in her eyes, but she blinked them back before she snapped. "You're just the same loser you were in high school that worked so hard to have everyone like him. You didn't belong then, and you sure as hell don't belong now. It's pathetic. You've never had a backbone, and right now, the only thing you're showing the Elders is just how weak and needy you are. You want their approval so badly that it's making you a coward."

Unable to control my rage any longer, I threw the glass of scotch across the room. Shards of glass flew everywhere, with amber liquid dripping from the wall. "Then let's call this off now," I boomed. "I don't need this shit."

Her eyes widened, but she didn't move from her place on the bed. "We can't. We have to finish."

"I don't fucking need the money or the stress. And you don't need the money either. So the fact that we're torturing ourselves right now seems pointless. I'm done." I began pacing the room, feeling like a caged tiger. "You're right about one thing. I have been trying to please the Elders, because that is the *fucking point* of the Trials. But I'm done. I've maxed out. Let's call it."

"Wait!" She held out a hand. "We can't just quit."

I smirked. "Yes, we can."

Bellamy took a deep breath. "We have to finish. We can't be quitters."

"Yes... we can."

The reality of walking out the door of the Oleander hit

me. Would I disappoint my father by not becoming a member of the Order? Possibly. Would it be a scandal or a shame? I supposed so. But Sully didn't pass the Trials, and he didn't become a member of the Order, and the world didn't come to an end. So why did I care so much?

I didn't need the Order for my business, my wealth, or my social standing. I had all that on my own. So why the fuck would I continue to put myself through this?

And the sick fact was that Bellamy was right. I was trying so damn hard to be the perfect overachiever like I had my entire life that it became all consuming.

Well, no more. I didn't have to do this. And I didn't have to stand here locked up in a damn cell with a woman who never liked me.

"Emmett," Bellamy said in a much calmer voice. In fact, it almost seemed like she had let go of all her anger. "I mean... we have permanent markings of the Order now. And we've been here for so long as it is. It would be a shame for all that to happen for nothing."

"Yeah," I said, nodding. "It was a waste of time."

I paused and took in her beauty. Even in her most simple attire, anger blotching her face and neck, and her hair disheveled, I had never seen a more stunning woman. "You know what the sad thing is? I really thought you and I had something forming. I really saw the possibility that you and I could...." I shook my head, hating that I was showing all my cards. "It doesn't matter now. As you pointed out, you are old money, and I'm new money. Our worlds will never be one."

Without saying another word, I turned to the door and left. I could hear Bellamy calling out my name, but I was beyond discussing this further. I was done being a people pleaser. I was done trying to prove myself to others. Done.

12

BELLAMY

That selfish son of a bitch. That night he walked out the door two weeks ago, I didn't even know if he left the Trials for good or if he was coming back. I barely slept at all, and him waltzing back in the next morning didn't make things any better.

Because... did he apologize? Acknowledge he'd been an ass or try to work things out with me *at all*?

No. No, he did not. He just sat down at his desk in the corner and opened his laptop, looking totally fresh and completely unperturbed. He barely even looked my way, like *he* was the one who had the right to be pissed off at *me*.

Well, I wasn't the queen bitch of my high school for nothing. He thought he could ice me out?

Ha.

I was the ice master.

So the next two weeks were quite... cold between us.

He wouldn't give. I wasn't about to budge. So we settled into a cool politeness. And the Elders were apparently on vacation, because it had been a dry spell in terms of Trials too.

Which was fine. Totally fine with me. Great, actually. I was just putting in my time here, and every day that passed was one more off the ticking clock.

Totally, totally *fine.*

Okay... well, maybe if I was being honest with myself...

I was about to climb the damn walls. I'd never been so bored, or felt so claustrophobic or so horny or frustrated and angry and furious, or wanted to *punch* things—and there'd been a lot of times in my life when I'd wanted to punch things.

Mainly my dad, after he was dead. But, ya know, that wasn't copacetic to say once someone was dead.

But I didn't learn just how bad he'd screwed Mom and me until then, and I couldn't even punch the bastard. I might've been mad at him for that most of all. Living any damn way he pleased and then just ducking out before he ever had to face any of the consequences. Talk about a *coward.*

They were all the same, weren't they?

I narrowed my eyes on Emmett, working away in the corner like always, when a knock came at the door.

I leapt off the bed if only for something to do and opened the door to Mrs. H. Her face was pale, and she tried for a pleasant smile as she handed a box to me.

"Good luck, dear," she said and then turned and hurried away down the hall.

Well, crap, if that wasn't ominous. It was probably just my imagination, but it was like I could feel the residual sting of the tattoo on my hip. It had healed up well, all things considered, but I was still pissed to have their permanent mark on me. It wasn't like I had money to get it lasered off.

Even if I passed the Trials, I understood the worth of money now and wouldn't waste it on frivolous shit ever again. No, this was all going to pay debts, and whatever was left would go to stocks and bonds so Mom and I would never have to worry about getting kicked out of our own house ever again. Only the bank knew how close we were to foreclosure due to non-payment of mortgage and property taxes.

I clutched the box to my chest. It was larger than normal but not too heavy. Was that a good or bad sign?

Which was why I *would* succeed at tonight's Trial and any one after it that they threw at us. In *spite* of my partner if I had to.

Emmett had at least turned away from his laptop to look at me. "Anything in the box?"

I pulled off the lid, and despite my determination to succeed no matter what, I couldn't say my stomach didn't drop out at seeing what was inside.

I pulled out the thick headband with long, pointed silver antlers attached to it. My eyes shot to Emmett as he stood up. I watched his Adam's apple bob as he looked at the antlers and briefly met my eyes.

But then he was all business again, squaring his shoulders. "Well, I guess this means there will be a hunt tonight."

I couldn't help the noise that escaped my throat—something between dismay and shock. A hunt? They were going to... to fucking *hunt* me?

"Maybe it's not what it seems?" I prompted, running a thumb over the realistic-looking antler. "It could be just a fetish thing."

"Sure," he said, then turned away from me toward the closet. "Either way, you better start getting ready."

"Oh right." I laughed caustically. "How could I forget? It's all about the show."

I started toward the bathroom, but he caught me by the forearm, his eyes dark. "Don't start with me tonight."

I yanked my arm away from him. "I can play if you can. Just don't expect me to call you Sir," I said, all but baring my teeth at him.

He just shook his head at me, his jaw taut. "Go," he ordered, pointing toward the bathroom.

I backed away from him. "I was already going. And not because you told me to!" I let the bathroom door slam behind me.

In spite of what Emmett said about a hunt, I thought he'd just been trying to rile me up. Until the Elders led us outside.

Late November in Georgia still felt like summer most nights, but still. I was naked. In addition to the antlers, they'd given me some slippers made out of what felt like deer-hide, but that was it. The antlers weren't very heavy on my head—they weren't plastic but were made of some other light material—and the headband cinched tight to keep them in place. But they were still awkward, and I had no idea how the hell I was supposed to *run* with them on.

The wind blew as I followed the lead Elder down the stairs of the front walk of the mansion, Emmett and the rest of the Elders at my back. I shivered unwillingly as I glanced up and all around. There was a half moon, but my eyes hadn't adjusted after the bright lights of the mansion to be able to make out much of anything more than the driveway and the shapeless blur of the field leading toward the lake and the forest beyond.

More than anything, I wanted to wrap my arms around

myself, but that felt like giving in somehow. Any show of weakness in front of the group at my back seemed like a bad idea. Already, there was anticipation in the air.

Anticipation for the hunt.

I could feel loose rocks underneath my feet, and my jaw locked. The slippers were a joke. They'd be useless against the sticks and brambles in the forest.

Once we all made it down the stairs and onto the driveway, the lead Elder banged his cane on the cobblestones.

"Welcome to the Silver Stag Hunt," he bellowed. "And what an exquisite little stag we have to chase tonight. Quite a luscious flank on her."

He reached over and caressed a hand over my ass, squeezing so hard I yelped and danced forward, making him and others in the crowd laugh.

The Elder banged his cane again until everyone quieted. "Standard hunt rules apply. If our little Silver Stag can evade capture until morning, she goes free. Otherwise, once captured"—the Elder grinned, looking me straight in the eye—"then all Hunters who desire will share the spoils."

I stumbled back a few steps.

"I for one," he said, eyes following me with a leer, "have had a hunger for some luscious little Stag ass that I've been wanting to slake for some time."

I trembled under his dark look. Dear God. This man had been one of my father's *friends*. I looked over his shoulder to where Emmett stood, but his face was emotionless as he stared at the ground.

Right. He wasn't going to stand up for me in front of these men whose respect he was so hungry for.

And me?

I had no choice.

No choice but to face what the night had in store for me.

"So you better start running, little Stag," the Elder finished in a whisper, reaching out and caressing a hand down my cheek. I pulled back and managed to stop short of spitting in his face. These men still held my future in their hands. I had to play along.

"How long of a head start do I have?" I managed to collect myself enough to ask.

"Less and less every moment you stand here asking stupid questions," he answered.

So I pivoted and sprinted away into the darkness.

13

BELLAMY

I'd grown up going to cotillion. Taking etiquette lessons. Learning how to flatter and banter. And I knew how to execute a perfect curtsey, for God's sake.

But sprinting through the woods essentially barefoot while trained hunters tracked me? Yeah, it wasn't high on my list of skills I'd gathered in my short life.

I was what you called an *indoor* girl. Even when I went "camping" growing up, it was *glamping*. My mother refused to go anywhere without running water and electricity for her curling iron.

So I ran away from the lake, because the lawn was mowed that direction, and I'd be easy to spot in so much open space. Which took me around back of the mansion, where I ended up running past a cemetery. A cemetery! As if I wasn't creeped out enough by the whole night and the thought that when I was inevitably captured, I'd be fucked by a train of dudes. Not even strangers—men I'd known my entire life!

I'd never been much of a sprinter, but I found myself

spurred on by the thought. I ran past the cemetery and into the woods.

But just like I expected, the stupid slippers were no match for the rugged terrain. Plus, the antlers kept getting caught in the branches. I had one hand up holding them on and another at my ankle trying to hold the slipper on as I stumbled through the forest.

My eyes were adjusting to the limited light, but Jesus, they were probably coming after me by now, and it would be over almost as soon as it started if I kept going like this.

I looked all around me at the strange forest. Maybe I could climb a tree, try to wait it out? But all the trees around me were pine, and the branches didn't start for about eight feet up. My stomach sank, and I could have cried.

But I'd learned long ago that curling up and crying did nothing. That was my mother's solution. Endless months locked away in her room. Wasting away, not eating unless I forced her to. The dead-eyed look of a woman who'd given up.

Coming home from school that day to find her passed out lifeless on the floor, pills scattered all around her.

I clenched my jaw.

Never.

I'd never give up.

So I forgot about trying to hold onto the stupid slippers and just ran. I ran through the woods even though rocks and sticks sliced at the tender soles of my feet, slippers long gone.

I forced the pain from my head, and I shoved branches out of the way. I pushed on when I had no more push left in me.

And when I heard noises behind me, the call of voices and a sharp whistle, I ran harder still.

They were gaining on me.

I couldn't keep this up. They had real shoes. I looked all around and, in the distance, something glinted. Goddammit, it was the lake.

But from the noise behind me, I had to assume most of them were in the forest. They obviously knew this was where I was.

And really, what was there to lose?

So I headed for the glint. Getting out of the forest was a relief even as I felt a double rush of freedom from the claustrophobia of the woods as well as anxiety at being out in the open.

At least from here, the lake wasn't far. I wouldn't be exposed for long. One quick look behind me showed no one was following me yet. I dropped to my knees and climbed the last few feet to the lake and slipped into the cool water.

I was overheated from my nonstop sprint, so crawling through the muddy water at the lake's edge felt good but shockingly cold at the same time. I blinked against it but didn't stop scrambling into the water.

When all of a sudden, the bank underneath my legs dropped out. I'd been planning to just... I don't know... wade in and stay on my hands and knees—definitely where I could touch. It hadn't been much of a plan to start with, but—

But as I flailed in the water, I didn't give a shit about stealth anymore. I couldn't touch the bottom. Oh shit, I couldn't touch the bottom!

I swallowed more water, coughed, and just ended up swallowing more. Oh shit, oh shit, where was the bottom? I struck out with my legs, but all I felt was reeds and other lake-bottom plants. The more I kicked, the more tangled I got.

I splashed and dipped under the surface, my hair and the goddamned antlers dragging me down. I screamed into the water, but more just went down my throat. Why the hell hadn't I ever learned to properly swim? Why did I think coming to the lake was a good idea, when I couldn't...?

What the fuck had I been thinking? I was going to die! I was going to die over a stupid, twisted fucking game.

Panicked, I splashed to the surface and barely sucked in a breath before I was going down again, down, down, down.

Well, he'd finally done it.

My father was going to end up killing us all in the end, wasn't he?

14

EMMETT

I couldn't run fast enough.

No matter how much I willed my legs to speed up, I had to instead watch Bellamy's head plunge beneath the water.

She was going to die if I didn't get there in time. I could see it all happening from a distance, and I worried I was too far away to reach her in time. But as I dove into the lake, reaching her body beneath the water, I was relieved to see her still struggling with the reeds that held her down below.

She was alive. She was fighting.

Yanking her away from the lake's hold, I swam us to the surface and then to the shore, both gasping for air as we reached the safety of the lake's edge.

I took her face into my hands so I could look into her eyes. "Are you okay?" I wiped the wet strands of hair off her face so I could make sure she didn't bang her head or get cut from being trapped beneath.

She began to cry but nodded. "I thought I was going to die. I would have if you—"

"Shh," I soothed as I pulled her into my arms. "You're safe now." Her body trembled next to mine. "But we need to get you inside and warmed up."

She was completely naked, her antlers long gone in the lake, and I had nothing of warmth to offer her, since I was just as wet as she was.

"I've never been so scared," she cried, clinging to my body.

"I know." I kissed the top of her head, rubbing her back as she shook within my arms. "But it's over now, and I'm going to keep you safe."

"I still have to hide. The hunt is—"

"It's over," I snapped. "This has gone too far when it came this close to claiming your life."

"Well, well," a voice from behind me said. "It appears you've found our stag."

I turned to see the Elders standing behind me with smiles of victory painted all over their wrinkled and fucked-up faces.

"She almost drowned," I said as I pulled both Bellamy and me to a standing position. We were soaked and muddy, and I had zero patience left. "Consider this Trial over."

"The rules are simple," an Elder said. "If we hunt her down before dawn, then she is ours to share."

"She didn't get hunted down," I answered through a clenched jaw. "She was rescued. By me. If I hadn't reached her in time, you all would have a dead body on your hands to deal with tonight."

Although, the minute I said the words, I realized Bellamy probably wasn't the first dead body they had to deal with in their time of being in the Order. With how dangerous some of these Trials were, there was no way no deaths occurred. Though the Elders had the power and resources to take care of the situation when it did.

"Rules are meant to be followed," another Elder said as he scanned Bellamy's body from head to toe. "Who wants the first taste?"

I felt her body tense next to mine, but she remained quiet, still regaining her breath as she panted for air.

"I'm taking her inside to get warm before she becomes hypothermic." I turned with her by my side, my arm securely around her, and didn't stop to hear their rebuttal.

"Emmett—"

"This conversation is over," I said with my back still to them, walking away. "Bellamy and I have completed each Trial of yours flawlessly. It's not our fault that this Trial was not conducted properly. You put her life at risk, and rather than making an issue of calling the Order out on their carelessness, I'm choosing to take my Belle inside."

I seriously doubted that my actions would lead to us failing the Initiation, but even if that were the case, then so be it. A woman nearly died tonight, and the last thing I was going to allow was for her to be sexually assaulted on top of it all.

And the truth...

It made me sick thinking of another man touching her.

No... she was mine. Even if it was temporary while we were here, and even if we could barely look at each other for the past weeks... she was still mine, and I was never going to allow any harm to come to her.

"Thank you," she finally said as we entered our room.

"I ran as fast as I could—"

"Not just for saving my life," she interrupted, "but for standing up for me. No one has ever stood up for me in my life. Ever. They were all going to rape me if you hadn't stepped in."

"I would never let that happen. Ever. No one is going to touch you but me."

I reached for a blanket but then realized a hot shower would be better, considering she was chilled to the bone and covered in mud. Without saying a word, I led her to the bathroom and turned on the faucet. As the water was heating up, I shed my own soaked and dirty clothes, knowing I had to warm up just as much as she did.

"Come on," I said, reaching for her hand as I tested the temperature of the shower. "Let's wash this awful night away."

She paused for a moment, her shivering body appearing so small and frail, as if she were deciding if she wanted to be in such an intimate situation with me. But before I had to insist, she took my hand and allowed me to guide her beneath the streaming water.

We both stood, body to body, beneath the warmth as the grime of the lake and shore flowed off our skin. Bellamy's lip trembled, and I could see tears welling in her eyes.

Wrapping my arms around her, I said, "It's okay to cry, if you need to. You went through an extremely traumatic event."

She shook her head as the hot water sprayed all around us. "I refuse to let them break me. I refuse to be one of their fucking broken belles. I'm not weak."

Tightening my arms around her, I replied, "You are far from weak. You are one of the strongest women I know. But right now, this very second, away from the judging eyes of the Elders, you can let down that shield. It's okay not to be—"

"I'm fine," she said as her voice broke. "I—"

She leaned her forehead against my chest and began to sob.

"It's okay," I soothed, knowing she had to get it all out. I couldn't imagine how scared she must have been, and as the adrenaline left her body, I was pretty sure that the reality of tonight had to be like a punch to the gut with how close she came.

"I don't know how my life got so fucked up," she mumbled against my wet skin between her sobs.

"You have a good life. Just remember—"

"No," she cut in. "My life is so messed up. It always has been."

I knew she was upset and had every right to be emotional. Rather than playing down her feelings and beliefs, I instead reached for the shampoo and began lathering it in her hair. She tensed at first but then practically melted into my arms as I washed every sign of tonight down the drain.

"Do you think the Elders are going to fail us? Do you think we'll be asked to leave?" Bellamy finally asked as her tears subsided, and her body stopped trembling.

I finished rinsing out the conditioner in her hair and reached for the body wash to rub over her skin, now that she seemed more accepting of my touch.

"No. I think they know we've done a good job up until now. My father is a member the Elders respect, and there is some power I have because of that too. Plus, there is no way that other Initiates haven't resisted Trials before. I would say we are due some grace. And even if they do kick us out, it's not like either of us really *need* this. We are fortunate enough to be in control of our own destinies."

Bellamy tensed and stepped away from the stream of water. I wasn't sure if it was the talk of the Elders or the fact that I had just caressed her body with soap, but I got the feeling she'd had enough of our shower.

Turning off the water, I reached for two towels and handed her one. "I'll start us a fire, and we can crawl into bed and warm up."

She didn't say anything more as she seemed melancholy but calm. At least she wasn't crying anymore, and she was warm in the safety of our room.

When we entered the bedroom, we were greeted with a teakettle and teacups waiting for us. Mrs. H must have gotten wind of what happened and wanted to offer us some of her comfort and support. I poured Bellamy a cup as she quickly dressed herself. Pulling on my own sweatpants, I then made my way over to the fireplace to warm our room even more.

"I don't want to fight anymore while we're here," she said softly behind me.

Stacking wood inside the hearth, I nodded. "I don't want to either. It got ugly, and I apologize for that. I said some pretty cruel things that you didn't deserve."

"We both said things we shouldn't have."

"And you were right," I confessed as the fire ignited. I walked back to the bed and crawled in beside her. "I am a perfectionist. I do care what people think. I'm an over-achiever to the point of it being a sick obsession at times. And I know I was pulling you into that addiction of mine. For that, I'm also sorry."

"I've had to be perfect my entire life," she said as she drank the last of her tea and put down her cup. "So I understand."

"But I shouldn't have been one of those people in your life. I shouldn't have expected you to be anything but the Bellamy that I... that I care for. You are perfect. You don't need to try."

I didn't mean for my confession to flow so easily from my tongue, but now that I admitted my truth, there was no turning back.

Bellamy studied my face for several moments and then said, "You don't need to be someone you aren't around me, Emmett. I like the man you are. Just the way you are."

She reached for the empty teacup on the nightstand and poured me some. Handing it to me, she asked, "Truce? No more battling each other. Let's battle our enemies together from now on."

Taking a sip of the tea, I watched the fire lick the wood in a mesmerizing way. "Truce. We're almost done with the Trials. I think ending them as a team is wise. We've gone through hell to get this far, and we're close to it all being over." I placed the cup down and turned my body to face her.

I considered kissing her. God, I wanted to kiss her.

But I didn't want to push too hard. She went through a lot tonight, and I didn't want to turn the night to be about me and my needs. It was about Bellamy and her feeling safe again. At least with me. I wanted her to feel safe with me.

"It hasn't been all hell," she said with a big yawn. "I'm glad I got to meet the real Emmett. Not the boy from high school, or the rich businessman I only see at social events. I'm glad to have finally met *you*."

"I'm glad I chose you, Bellamy. I don't think I've told you that before, and I know I definitely haven't always shown it. But I'm really glad it was you I chose."

She smiled warmly and snuggled down in her pillow, pulling the blankets up around her chin. She yawned again as her eyes grew heavy. "Goodnight, Emmett. I'm glad you chose me too."

15

BELLAMY

The next morning, all my limbs were sore, and my head felt thick, like I'd been out partying the night before.

"Morning, sleepyhead," Emmett said when I turned over and rubbed at my eyes. He was in bed beside me with his laptop, smiling down at me.

My heart did a weird fluttery thing at him being there instead of at his desk.

I looked around, still squinting. "What time is it?"

"Almost ten."

I scooted up to a sitting position, pushing my hair back from my face. "Oh my God. I can't believe I slept so long."

He closed his laptop. "You needed the rest. I told Mrs. H to hold breakfast for us."

"Oh." I blinked, pulling up one of my legs to my chest and circling it with my arms. "Thanks."

"You hungry?"

I thought about it for a second and then nodded vigorously. Come to think of it, I was starving.

"Great." He stood. "I'll let her know we're coming while you get dressed."

I nodded, still a little stunned by his solicitousness after our two-weeks-long cold war. He disappeared from the room, and I hurried into the bathroom.

Ten minutes later, we were seated in the breakfast nook that overlooked the grounds, with Mrs. H serving up scones and Devonshire cream. "Eggs and bacon will be up shortly," she said, and Emmett nodded.

"Thanks." I reached for a scone, feeling timid, which was very unlike me.

After Mrs. H hustled back out again, I looked over the table at Emmett. He looked crisp and put together, like always. He was in a pressed button-up shirt and slacks—Armani by the look of it.

I'd just pulled on a shirt and leggings. I reached for a scone and picked it apart on my plate. "So um, I'm not sure if I said it last night, since everything feels like a blur." I looked into his eyes. "But thanks. Thank you. I really mean it. It, um…" I dropped my eyes to my plate and cleared my throat. "It meant a lot that you stood up for me like that. And for saving my life too, obviously."

My cheeks flamed hot as I looked back up at him. "You're worth standing up for."

Goddammit. He was going to make me cry.

He didn't seem embarrassed or awkward though. I took several long swallows of my orange juice to cover getting my emotions back under control. Jesus, what? I had *one* near-death experience, and now I was a wimpy cry-baby? Was that it?

I shook my head and sat up straighter. "Anyway, I just appreciate it. So thank you."

He smiled at me, and for once, I let myself stare at him.

"You're so different than I thought you'd be."

He rolled his eyes, and his jaw went a little tense. "So I've finally convinced you I'm not a groveling little boy hungry for everyone else's approval after all?"

I breathed out. "Okay, I deserved that."

But he shook his head quickly. "I'm sorry. We cleared the air last night. I'm not one to hold grudges."

To which I laughed out loud. "Aren't you? It's okay. I respect a good grudge."

The corners of his lips turned up. "I might have made some snap judgments about you over the years too."

"So tell me about who you are now. I've met Emmett the Master. But not Emmett the *man*. What do you, like, *do* in your spare time?" I popped a big bite of scone in my mouth as he shrugged.

"What's there to tell? I work with my father running a multinational renewable energy company."

"And you love it, don't you? You were always geeking out about math and science stuff growing up, if I remember correctly."

His brow furrowed a little. "You noticed what I was into back then?"

I rolled my eyes. "I mean, you always had that Rubik's cube with you. And you did math competitions or something?"

He ruefully admitted, "I was a State Mathlete finalist my last three years of high school."

I laughed out loud. "Exactly."

"What can I say?" He rolled his eyes. "I knew how to impress the chicks."

"High school girls are idiots. Including me." I looked him in the eye as I said it and hoped he could understand what I wasn't saying.

I knew I'd been a bitch to him back in the day. It had never been about him. He wasn't the only one who could obsess about how things looked on the outside. There was a time when I'd been so desperate to keep up appearances that being thought of as a bitch was infinitely preferable to the pity and scorn I might've faced if anyone knew the truth. It was the only defense mechanism of a scared teenage girl.

I opened my mouth to try to explain some of this to him, but he was already talking.

"Yeah, well, it's not a problem anymore. Now, I have the opposite problem."

I frowned. "What do you mean?"

He gave a long-suffering sigh. "You know Darlington mothers. Do you know how many Sunday brunches I've sat through that are such obviously desperate setups to pair off their gold-digging daughters? It's not just here. In Atlanta, the women learn my last name and only see dollar signs." His mouth turned down. "It's disgusting."

I nodded, feeling my cheeks warm again as I shoved my mouth full of more scone. "That must suck."

He nodded, looking distantly toward the window. "My mom met my dad before the money, when he was just an MIT grad struggling to pay off his student loans. It's one of the things I've always been jealous of. He knows she loves him just for *him*, ya know?" His eyes came back to me, and I nodded, mouth still full.

"That's so rare in the world we live in. All these people here—" He gestured around us, and I knew he meant the opulence we found ourselves in. "—it's all so fake. They're just using each other like it's a transaction."

I swallowed down the scone, then reached for my juice again. After taking another long sip, I looked back at him. "I can't even imagine the kind of relationship your mom and dad have. It's completely different from the way I grew up with my parents. I mean, I like to think that at one time they at least *liked* each other..." My voice drifted off. "But by the end—" I shook my head. "—I mean, he traveled so often for business I barely ever saw him."

"I'm sorry. And I'm sorry for your loss. He died a few years ago, right?"

I shook my head, denying his sympathy. "It's fine. He wasn't that great of a guy." Understatement of the century.

"Anyway, I was groomed to be just like my mom. To be the perfect debutante so I could capture the perfect man. The culture down here is messed up."

"So is that why you're doing this?" he asked, and by the way his forehead was scrunched, I knew he was really curious. "As an F-U to that way of life, or what?"

"Something like that," I said, looking back down at my plate. Because as honest as we were being, pride was a hard thing to swallow.

The man sitting across from me was a *billionaire*. And was I going to sit here and admit I had nothing? *Less* than nothing? I didn't even have a college degree.

And I hadn't forgotten the disgust on his face when he talked just a minute ago about *gold-diggers*.

He respected me because he thought I was here on some sort of rebellious lark. He thought we were equals.

"Still going to play mysterious?" he prompted, and I didn't miss the frustration in his voice. But all I could do was pick up my scone, smile coyly, and shrug, while inside, a little more of me crumbled away.

∾

STILL, IT WAS A TURNING POINT. I WOULDN'T SAY WE WENT back to our old selves like we'd been before. No, we didn't go back to Master and submissive twenty-four seven.

But after his work was done, or during extended lunches, we would... *play*.

The next month passed far less painfully than I would have expected. There were a few Trials, but, and I don't know if the Elders had decided to take it easy on us after the last disastrous one or something—which didn't seem like a very Elder thing to do, but hey, I wasn't complaining—they weren't bad at all.

Going downstairs for some public orgies didn't really bother me. Especially when they seemed to turn Emmett on. As long as he wasn't expected to share me, his Dom self seemed to get off on the voyeuristic nature of showing off just how far he could push me—and make me beg for it.

And when things were good like this between us, *damn*, they were good.

During our first month and a half, I never knew if Emmett would want to pause work for meals, but ever since the Hunt, he always made time for them. Especially breakfast. Sometimes we'd spend a couple of hours in the breakfast nook chatting and reading parts of the paper to each other, doing the crossword together, laughing over the dumb comics. He was always sweet about the crosswords, which I bet he could do in his sleep, but he let me puzzle over the clues before suggesting an answer he'd probably known all along.

I never realized before getting to know Emmett that a man could be so *sweet* and also be the most badass, sexy, dominant lover I'd ever known.

This morning, for example.

I was sleepy. One thing I liked about being here was

sleeping in. Mom never let me sleep in at home, even though I was a grown-ass woman. She'd bang on my door at ungodly hours of the morning, wailing about how we didn't even have a woman to cook us *eggs* anymore and how we were *starving* now! And she'd keep it up until I dragged my ass out of bed and went downstairs to put on the coffee and make some sort of breakfast out of whatever was left in the pantry.

But I had to say, being woken by the gentlest kisses on the back of my neck was the kind of wake-up call I didn't mind.

It was full light out, so Emmett had given me time to sleep, even though I knew he liked to get an early start.

I smiled as I wiggled my tush back against him and—oh! I smiled even wider. Yes, somebody was *very* awake.

But when I tried to turn around to envelop him in my arms, he caught my wrists and urged me forward again, his chest still to my back. His arms came around me, hands on my wrists as both our arms hugged me, tucked close to my breasts until I was surrounded on all sides by him.

The head of his cock nudged between my legs, and I opened to him, my breath hitching as I did. Even after months, the feel of him still affected me so. There was no growing tired of this man. I couldn't imagine this ever getting old.

His hands clenched with pressure on my wrists as he thrust his hips forward, spearing into my pussy with one great thrust.

"You're so beautiful when you submit to me so completely like this," he said, clenching me to him tighter as he pulled out and then thrust back in again. "It makes me want to fuck you like a maniac, to take you to that place I know you love—when you're mindless and completely free in pleasure."

I could only grunt out a desperate, "*Please.*"

It was early morning still, and I was half-befuddled with sleep, but waking to this—my domineering master wanting to take me to the mountaintop with him as he played my slickened body like a maestro—oh God, yes, *please*, I wanted to go on the ride.

I could feel his grin from behind me by the way the hairs on the back of my neck stood up. And then his voice was a warm breath at my ear, both of us still on our sides.

"Your wish is my command."

He fucked me rapidly several more times and then slowly, so that both of us heard the noise of his cock sliding against the slick, slippery folds of my pussy. It was obscene. I squirted out more wetness, listening to us and feeling every inch of him inside me, dragging slowly, slowly, the fat ridge of his head hitting every delicious part of me along the way.

One of his hands let go of my wrist, and he reached down for my thigh, lifting it and bending my knee so I was even more exposed to his cock disappearing inside me.

He looked into my eyes as I watched him over my shoulder. When our eyes connected, he grinned. "Just remember you asked for this, Princess."

The next time he pulled out, he repositioned himself and then began pressing in again, but this time at a different hole.

I gasped and tensed in surprise.

"Relax," he said, kissing and then biting softly at the back of my neck. "You can take me. We both know you can take me. Relax and let me in. Submit and let me take control."

Submit. For a second, I clenched tighter, but then I

relaxed as he continued speaking, and I let myself get lost in the rich bass of his voice. The more I released, the more ground he took, pressing into me, claiming me.

And as I gave, the lightness came. As he filled me up from behind, it traveled through my entire groin, straight through to my clit, and my body sang as I clenched my legs together and shook, tremoring and clenching on Emmett's cock in my ass.

"Fuck, *yes,* that's right. Give in to me. Fucking milk my cock. Break my dick, princess. Holy *fuck,* that's so fucking tight. I can barely *move* you're so hot and tight. Hottest fucking thing I ever—"

His hand let go of my thigh but only to move to my sopping pussy. First, he just shoved more of my wetness back toward his cock as he continued to breach me.

And then those fingers moved, almost as if they couldn't help themselves. Even though I knew every move Emmett made was calculated, and this was probably only more of his torture, I loved this soft, investigative touch as he explored with first one thick, fat finger and then finally, *finally,* two.

But it wasn't until he dropped his palm hard against my clit with three fingers inside me that I lit up like the Fourth of fucking July.

I writhed, I screamed, and I humped Emmett's hand while he fucked my ass, and there were so many senses being stimulated at once.

The orgasm felt like it rippled outward from my *tailbone.* It almost hurt it hit so hard. And then it was fucking bliss. And Emmett wasn't about to let me off easy.

He made me ride it to another, fucking my ass raw, spreading me open and defiling me, blasting my pussy with his hand, and then digging his middle finger deep and circling round and round with the tip hooked on that spot that ohhh—

I think I screamed as the blinding white light hit. I breathed. Maybe I breathed. Who fucking cared? This was Nirvana, and I was gonna ride this wave, ride my man, both of us fucking each other like the animals we were. God, I couldn't get enough of fucking him. Oh God, it was so good. Oh God!

So, yeah. Ahem. That was this morning. And now it was tonight. But, Jesus. My legs still quivered just remembering it. That was before the box had come at breakfast. I was sure Emmett wouldn't have fucked me half so well or let me have nearly as many orgasms if he'd known, so I was a little smug about that.

Suffice to say, when Emmett and I weren't fighting, we worked out very, *very* well.

In the box for tonight, there was actually clothing for me, for once. Well, a slinky thigh-high silk robe anyway. It was still more than I usually got. Though, considering how things usually went, I doubted I'd be wearing it long.

Emmett was tense as we prepared to go downstairs.

"What's up with you?" I asked as we headed toward the door.

He shrugged. "Things have just been going smoothly for a while now. It puts me on edge."

I trailed a finger down the center of his shirt, along his tidily done buttons. "Don't be so serious."

His eyes were dark as he caught my wrist in a firm grip.

I smiled bigger. "See? You're in a mood to play after all."

He just shook his head, let go of my wrist, and gave me a

resounding smack on the ass that I felt long after we left the room and started heading down the stairs.

Downstairs, things weren't too much out of the ordinary. I wasn't the only girl in the room, which always made me feel better. Women were draped here and there over Elders throughout the crowd.

But when we were directed to sit on two chairs facing each other, my nerves did stir. It felt too much like the night we'd gotten tattoos, and if they tried to pull that shit again....

Emmett gave my forearm a squeeze before we were forced to part, directed to the large winged chairs set up in the center of the room across from one another.

Once we were seated, the rest of the crowd circled around us, and the Elders started banging those damnable canes of theirs.

Emmett sat ramrod straight, face impassive while he waited to hear what would be expected of us and I tried to do the same. I knew it was important to him to put on a good face in front of the Elders, and now that I knew he *would* stand up to them for me, I'd been trying my hardest to make him proud of me. I didn't give a shit what the Elders thought of me, as long as they passed me. But I'd try extra, for Emmett. So I sat up straight too and tried to be a perfect Belle.

"Welcome to tonight's game of Truth or Dare," said the Elder. "Let's see if our Initiate and his Belle squirm under the light of the Inquisition!"

Canes banged, and cheers went up from all around.

Truth or Dare? Were they serious? My eyes shot to Emmett. If anything though, he was smiling easier now, looking relaxed.

Because he didn't have any secrets he was keeping.

Shit.

I shifted uneasily in my seat and crossed my legs. I didn't have any *bad* secrets I was keeping. I mean, I hadn't really done anything wrong. I was just poor. That might be a crime in Darlington County in some people's eyes, but I didn't think Emmett would—

"Emmett, truth or dare?"

"Truth," he said, leaning back in his chair, his hands on the armrests as if it was a throne and he the king. That was how comfortable he looked here in this room among these men.

His peers.

His equals.

"Have you or your father ever cheated a business partner? Remember, if you lie here, it could result in your expulsion from the Trials."

My mouth went dry. Jesus, they weren't pulling any punches, were they? And asking about his business—was this some kind of fishing expedition?

Emmett's eyes searched the crowd and paused for a moment. He was looking past and behind me, so I couldn't see who he was looking at—his father, maybe?

Emmett then looked up at the Elder who'd asked the question. "I can only speak for myself and to the best of my knowledge for the company, but no, we have never cheated a business partner as far as I know."

Canes banged, and then the Elder turned to me. "Truth or dare, Ms. Carmichael?"

I swallowed again, then, before I could overthink it, I squeaked out, "Dare."

The man smiled at me, and it wasn't necessarily kind or pleasant. "I dare you to make out with Jenny over there while Elder St. Claire fucks her."

My eyes shot to Emmett, whose hands had clenched into

fists. Then I looked at the Elder. "Only make out with her? I don't have to touch *him*?"

"Only her."

I looked at Emmett again, and he gave the briefest of nods.

"All right. I accept the dare."

"Robe off," the Elder said as I stood.

I barely stopped myself from rolling my eyes as I untied the flimsy little silk ribbon holding the robe closed at my waist and opened it. A chaise had been dragged over so it was also center stage, and I saw Walker's dad drop his silver robe and stand at the end of it, fully erect. A woman—Jenny, I assumed—climbed up on her hands and knees.

I breathed out hard before I joined the tableau, lounging in front of Jenny. She smiled at me, not looking shy at all.

I would wait until—

But Mr. St. Claire wasted no time in grabbing her hips and burying himself inside her. He quickly took up a ball-slapping rhythm, fucking her from behind. Her tits swayed with the motion, and her fingers grasped the edges of the chaise.

"Now," the Elder behind me demanded.

I nodded and reached a hand forward, holding Jenny's face. It was soft. She was young, in her mid to late twenties. What had brought her here tonight?

No time to stop and ask. I leaned in and kissed her.

Her lips were soft, and she kissed me back, making pornographic noises that were clearly for the audience.

Fine with me.

I wondered if Emmett liked what he saw? Did it turn him on, seeing me kiss another woman? Thinking about that had me kissing her a little more enthusiastically, even if it was hard to maintain a kiss with her constantly bobbing forth and backward like this.

It only lasted a few more minutes anyway.

But she was kissing enthusiastically by the end, her tongue seeking its way around my mouth. She bit at my bottom lip when Mr. St. Claire reached around to rub her clit, and her noises turned genuine as she sucked on my lips and came.

I pulled back, blinking from an experience I could only call a first.

I was a little wobbly as I went back to my chair. *Okay, well, phew.* First dare, survived. I looked at Emmett, and his eyes were searing. I wasn't sure, but I thought he liked what he'd seen. He looked like that when he was horny. Which turned *me* on, so when I sat down, I was squirming for entirely different reasons than I had at the beginning of this challenge.

"Back to you," the Elder turned to Emmett. "Truth or dare?"

"Truth," Emmett said again.

"What's the one thing you hate people knowing about you?" the Elder asked, unflinching.

I flinched. Jesus. You didn't just go around asking people a thing like that.

I expected Emmett to switch to dare, but he just looked his examiner in the eye and answered. "I hate for people to know that I'm insecure about whether they'll ever like me for me or just for my money. I hate for them to know that deep down, I don't believe they would just like me for myself."

Holy *shit*. Did he really just admit that? Out loud to this room of vultures? And I'd once called him a coward. He was so goddamned brave.

I wanted to run over to him and tell him he was ridiculous. That anyone who really got to know him would lo—

I froze midthought.

Oh shit. They'd *love* him. Anyone who really got to know him would *love* him. Did that mean...? Was I saying that I...?

I blinked, almost missing the question when the Elder turned and asked me, "Truth or dare?"

"Oh... um, I...." I shook my head. "Dare."

"I dare you to bend over, hold onto that chair, and let any man in this room who wants to spank you."

Emmett stood up. "Can she change to truth?"

The Elder nodded. "She can."

I sat there squirming, looking between Emmett and the Elder, terrified of what he'd ask me. But if Emmett had been brave, maybe I could too?

"What's the truth question?" I asked.

"Why did your mother send you here?" The Elder looked me straight in the eye. "Remember, a lie disqualifies you."

My mouth dropped open before I slammed it shut. The sons of bitches! I could feel Emmett's eyes on me. Of course I could. He had no idea Mom had *sent* me here. I knew he expected me to keep my seat and calmly respond to their question.

But I panicked. "Dare."

So I stood up, moved around to the side of the chair, grasped the arm with my hands, and assumed the position.

16

EMMETT

"No. Truth," I snapped, narrowing my eyes on Bellamy, who avoided making eye contact with me. "She'll be taking *truth*."

This had nothing to do with another man being allowed to spank her at this point.

I wanted to hear the truth.

My gut screamed at me that I *needed* to hear the truth.

The Elders banged their canes on the ground, and the Elder leading the game said, "Truth, Bellamy. Sit down."

Bellamy visibly swallowed and inhaled deeply before following their order, her eyes downcast to her feet.

"Ms. Carmichael, I will repeat the question again. Why did your mother make you come to the Oleander? Why did she want you to be a Belle?"

I waited, my stomach tightening as I did. I could barely breathe as I watched the woman I lov— the woman I had grown to care about reveal a truth she clearly didn't want to tell.

"Let me remind you that not answering truthfully will result in failing the Trial," the Elder said.

Her eyes finally lifted to meet mine, and I saw sorrow dancing within them. She couldn't hold the stare with me for long and returned her glare to the ground once more.

"She wanted me to become a Belle in hopes that I would be chosen, so that I could seduce an Initiate into marrying me."

Her body trembled as she sat across from me, and although I didn't like her mother's intention, I wasn't exactly surprised by it either. Every single mother in Darlington was guilty of wanting or even trying to set their daughters up with me in hopes of engagement. It was our culture and in their blue-blooded nature. Every mother had the duty to find a man for their daughter with the same wealth—if not more—than their own lineage and the ability to provide a luxurious and respected lifestyle that matched their daughter's childhood. It didn't make sense why Bellamy would be so upset by admitting this.

"There's more," an Elder said as he slammed his cane into the marble floor.

Bellamy flinched but then added, "Everyone in his group who went through the Trials before Emmett have fallen in love with their belles and started a life with them. Marriage or the talks of marriage have come from the Trials. The end result is that every Belle gets a committed relationship."

The same Elder as before pounded his cane again. "There's more."

"She wants me to marry Emmett," Bellamy blurted out, her eyes still focused on her feet and not me sitting across from her.

"All right, Ms. Carmichael," the Elder said, "we will help you speed this truth process along. *Why* does your mother want you to marry Emmett?"

She finally looked up at me again. "For his money."

"There's more!" the Elder shouted with another pound of his cane.

Bellamy's eyes darted to the Elders and then to me. Her lips trembled, and she mouthed, "I'm sorry," to me before she answered, "Because my mother and I are broke. We've been broke for years and living a lie that we have money when we don't. My mother felt that if I married Emmett, our money issues would be solved. She wanted me to marry him for his money, because we *need* it."

I remembered when I tried to join the football team to blend in with Montgomery, Sully, and the rest of my friends. I had been tackled hard and nearly knocked out on my first catch. I can still remember the feeling of having the air knocked out of me and fearing that I would never be able to breathe again. Inhaling fresh air seemed impossible, and...

I was experiencing that feeling again now.

"What was your request at the end if you were to complete all the Trials?" the Elder asked.

"To have Emmett marry me," she answered quietly, tears welling in her eyes.

"Why wouldn't you just ask for a shitload of money like the rest of the whores do?" I boomed as I stood from my seat and hovered over her. "Why marriage?"

Bellamy looked up at me, the tears finally falling down her face. "Status," she answered simply. "We need more than just a paycheck. You know how Darlington works."

I needed air.

I needed fucking air.

I took a few large steps away from her and turned my back on everyone. "Yeah, I know exactly how Darlington is," I said more to myself than anyone else.

The Elders all began to bang their canes in unison,

signaling that the Trial was complete. They had achieved their goal for the evening.

Keeping my composure as best as I could in order to not show how absolutely devastated I was to hear Bellamy's truth, I took hold of her arm and helped her stand. I refused to show them that they had power over me. No one had power over me.

No one.

Not even Bellamy.

We exited the ballroom side by side, the same way we entered.

"Lift your fucking head up," I whispered between clenched teeth. "The Elders will not break us."

Bellamy immediately complied and pulled her shoulders back as she did.

When we entered our bedroom, she spun on her heels to face me the minute I closed the door.

"I'm so sorry, Emmett. I know what you must be thinking."

"That you're like everyone else," I began, marching straight to the whiskey bottle to pour myself a glass. "That I shouldn't be surprised by this."

She walked over to the closet and pulled on some clothing, oddly adding some normal to our anything-but situation. She remained quiet, but what more could she say? She had to show all her cards, and what a fucked-up deck she had.

"Bravo," I said as I took a large gulp of my drink. "I didn't see the game. I can usually spot when a woman is using me a mile away. You did a very good job at blinding me."

"It wasn't a game," she said softly. "I wasn't using you."

I huffed and walked over to the window, my back to her as I looked out onto the night's sky. "Not using me? Then what would you call it? Your request was to marry me at the end. Not money. Not using The Order for money. Not fucking them over. But fucking *me* over. Forcing *me* to marry *you*." I spun around to face her. "So tell me how that isn't using me."

"When I started all this... when I agreed to be a Belle, I didn't think the entire thing through. Not really. I mean... how could I? I was just doing what my mother expected, like I've done my entire life. I don't get the luxury in my life to say no. I don't get to live my life how I'd choose. I do what every good Southern Belle does and submit to the rules of society."

She sat down on the edge of the bed, fiddling with her fingers. "But you're right. I have been playing a game." She looked at me. "Ever since my father died, leaving us penniless, I've been playing it. Coming here was no different. Smoke and mirrors."

I chuckled, venom seeping out in the sound. "Smoke and mirrors. That's all you are. That's all you've ever been." Deciding to be truthful myself, I added, "I truly thought you were different. The Bellamy I got to know in this room... well, I thought you were different. I thought I got to know the *real* you."

"You did," she countered quickly. "Even though I hid my money—or lack of—from you, it doesn't mean I lied. I tried really hard to never actually lie to you. I didn't want you knowing the truth, just as I didn't want anyone knowing the truth. Do you know how embarrassing it is to be poor in Darlington when you were once rich? Do you know how hard it was to keep up appearances, to hide our truth from everyone? I was in high school and could barely afford lunches, let alone a prom dress, and I know I'm not the only girl with money issues. I'm not doing a 'poor me'—"

"It sure as fuck sounds like it," I retorted with a raise of my glass. "Poor little rich girl."

"I've gone my entire life trying to act and look like someone I'm not." She paused for a long moment and then said, "But with you, while we were here, I got to be me. I got to release the prissy beauty queen and just... live. I knew it would all come crashing down. I knew this little safe bubble we've been in would pop soon enough. But I have to be honest, Emmett. I've liked being here. I've liked the Trials... or most of them. I like the confinement in this room and being forced to spend every second with you."

Her face turned a shade of pink as she added, "And I really liked being submissive to you. I liked how you took control and how easy it was for me to give it to you. For the first time in my life, I feel as if I can finally breathe."

Walking over to the chair by the fireplace, I sat down. "Let me ask you something." I took a sip of my whiskey and motioned for her to take a seat across from me.

She tentatively did so, and as she approached, I could see her hands were shaking. A self-destructive part of me wanted to take her into my arms to help calm her nerves. There was a protective urge inside me to care for this woman. To guarantee that all would be fine and I'd fix all her problems.

But I wasn't a damn fool. Not anymore.

"How did you know I'd choose you?" I asked.

"Because." She swallowed hard. "I knew you had a crush on me in high school. I've also seen you watching me at other social engagements the past couple of years. I knew... or at least I hoped...."

"So if you knew it would be so easy to wrap me around your finger, why not just work your Darlington magic with your mother and get me to marry you like all the other gold-diggers do?"

"Because it's *you*, Emmett. You wouldn't agree to that. You were never going to marry any woman in Darlington, and you know it."

"And why is that?" I asked, my voice rising a little higher than intended.

"What do you mean?" Bellamy's eyes locked with mine.

"Why wouldn't I marry anyone in Darlington?"

I saw the realization enter her eyes as she licked her lips and nodded. She took a deep breath. "Because you've always felt used for your money. That no one genuinely would love you if it weren't for your money. That—"

"Exactly!" I shouted, slamming my empty glass down on the end table and standing. "I would never marry a money-hungry whore unless forced. You knew this. You knew this and used this against me."

She flinched when I used the word "whore," and though I hated losing my control and composure, calling her something I didn't mean, I couldn't help it. I wanted to hurt her. I wanted to make her feel the pain I was feeling. I wanted her to feel dirty and used like I did. I wanted her... to be different.

I truly thought she was different.

"I know you're angry," she began, standing up to join me.

"I'm not angry," I said. "I'm sickened. I'm sick and tired of all this." I lifted my arms and motioned around the room. "I've tried so fucking hard to be respected, to be one of the Southern elites. I've wanted to be perfect at everything. And for what? For this? What the fuck is this?"

She didn't say anything but took a step toward me, her wide eyes pleading for me to understand.

"And after all the shit we've been through for this Initiation, we will ultimately fail. We are so close to the end, and now we have to walk away as losers."

"We don't have to fail," she answered.

I laughed almost maniacally. "Oh but we do. Because no way in hell would I ever allow you to get your wish. I won't marry you, Bellamy. I won't ever marry someone who wants nothing more from me than my money."

"I don't want you for your—"

"But you do," I interrupted. "And no matter what, I refuse to be used."

I watched tears fall down her cheeks, and there was still an almost consuming need to wipe them from her cheeks and pull her into my arms. I wanted to smell the floral essence from her hair as I kissed her worries away. I wanted to—

Fuck that.

"Don't cry, Bellamy. You're a beautiful woman and will be able to land some other poor fool who will be your sugar daddy."

"Please don't be mean," she said in barely a whisper. "And that's not what I want."

The thought of her being with another man was more *mean* to me than it was to her. It made me physically ill, and I considered throwing up the whiskey I just drank in hopes of getting rid of this ball of tension in my gut.

Hating that I could feel my heartbeat in my temples and worried I might say or do something I'd regret, I stormed to the door to leave.

"Emmett, please don't go. Can we talk this out?"

I looked over my shoulder. "I really thought you were different, Bellamy. Thank you for finally opening my eyes tonight."

17

BELLAMY

Obviously, it was a terrible secret, and terrible for it to come out that way, but if he would have just let me explain....

Or maybe there was no explaining it away. The truth was I'd gone back and forth about what I was going to ask for at the end of the Trial. Sometimes, I thought I'd be bolder and ask just for the money, and Emmett would never have to know about the other. Things seemed to be going so well between us naturally that I... I hadn't wanted to think about the end. That was what I did, right? Live in the moment so hard I could pretend I wasn't constantly just dancing right on the knife's edge of collapse? Ignoring tomorrow was a way of life for me.

I spent the night crying and pacing and waiting for Emmett to come back, and then just after dawn, there was a knock at the door. My heart leapt. Was it Emmett, finally ready to talk to me? We'd had fights before, and surely if he'd just....

But when I rushed to the door and yanked it open, it was only Mrs. H on the other side, with a breakfast tray in her hands. "Oh. It's you." My shoulders slumped, and I turned away from her.

"Well, I won't take that as an insult, considering all I heard happened in the ballroom last night. She set the breakfast service on a side table. "Come here, dearie. Do you need a hug?"

My first instinct was to lash out. No, I didn't need a fucking hug! I didn't need anything from anybody!

But then I looked toward the older woman with the kind laugh lines on her face and couldn't hold back. I went forward and collapsed into her arms. She was warm and soft, and dammit, she gave great hugs.

"There, there, dearie, it'll be all right in the end," she said, patting my back.

She was so nice and motherly.

Motherly in a way my own mother had never been.

I broke down sobbing into her overlarge bosom, and she held me closer still. "That's right, lassie. Let it out. Let it all out."

So I did. I cried and cried, and once I was all cried out, I slumped back from her and collapsed down on the bed, curling up sideways with a pillow to my chest. Mrs. H sat down beside me and rubbed my back.

"How are you so good at this?" I asked. "Do you have kids?"

A slightly sad look crossed her face. "None of my own. But the members' children have grown up around the Oleander. I feel like I've had a hand in raising so many of these boys."

I swiped at my eyes. "So why don't you hate me? Trying to trap one of them into marrying me?"

Mrs. H looked down at me, pulling her hand away from my back. "Well, I had my suspicions in the beginning; I won't deny it. I'm protective of my boys, especially knowing what your ask was." She shook her head. "But then I watched the two of you together. And I have to say, that boy's usually so serious he's like a little old man. Except when you're around. He lights up and acts his age. He remembers there's more to life than work and trying so hard to be accepted into certain realms of society. He remembers that he deserves to have joy and companionship."

I swallowed hard. "But I ruined everything. I just... I didn't know how to tell him."

"Tell him what?"

"What it was really like growing up. In high school at least, I mean."

"Why don't you start by telling me?"

I huffed out and swiped at my eyes, but it wasn't the worst idea I'd ever heard. My secret was out anyway. Obviously, all the men in the Order knew my circumstances, and they were the most important men in town. What reputation was I trying so hard to protect with my silence anymore?

"It started right after Daddy died. Mama and I found out he had a gambling problem. A bad one. We were in terrible debt, and there was nothing—no money, no bonds, and barely any assets to pay it off."

Mrs. H's hand went to her chest. "Oh, honey. What on earth did you do?"

I shook my head. "At first, nothing. Mom was in denial. I was a sixteen-year-old brat, used to having everything on a whim, having my meals prepared by a cook and everything cleaned up by a maid. They were the first to go, obviously. When the first debt collector showed up at the door...."

Well, that night, I'd walked in and found my mother on the floor with the pills sprawled all around her. Terrified, I dragged her limp body over to the toilet and shoved my finger down her throat until she started gagging and then throwing up. The pills she spewed into the toilet still looked mostly whole, so apparently I'd gotten there right in time.

I'd wanted to take Mom to the hospital, but she'd gotten desperate, saying no, we didn't have the money. She was sorry, she'd sobbed; she'd never do it again. She'd been weak.

"Did things get better?" Mrs. H asked after I gave a quick overview of Mom's first attempt.

I shook my head with a sigh. "I wish. No, every time things got harder, I had to go on Mom-watch. When the red notices started showing up for the house, I came home and found her in the bathtub, trying to slit her wrists with dull razor blades. There were shallow cuts all up and down her arm, she just hadn't been able to bring herself to commit. It was right around senior prom, I think. On the outside, I was barely keeping my shit together, but it was this part I was playing now.

"My real life was home with this broken woman, trying to keep her from offing herself while our world fell down around us. And during the day, I played at being a bitchy teen girl, this fictional version of my former self. But I clung to it even harder, because somehow, if no one knew what was happening at home, it was like it wasn't real. Like I wasn't sleeping at the foot of Mom's bed because I knew her depression got worse at night and if I was there, I could keep her from trying to take matters into her own hands.

"The hours at school, I was constantly worried about what I might find when I went home. And every day I found her alive was both a victory, and it also meant another exhausting night keeping her that way."

"Oh, honey," Mrs. H interjected. "How did you manage to go on like that? You were just a child."

"Well, I couldn't stay one for long, could I? I dragged my mom into the bank and forced her to face renegotiating the loan and consolidating the loan on the house. It meant we were mortgaged up to our eyeballs and couldn't leave the property even if we wanted to. But as long as we paid a little each month, we were able to stay there."

"Okay, that's great," Mrs. H said. "So you found a solution."

"It was just a short-term solution, and only because my father had been part of the Order. The banker we went to was a fellow Order member, and the deal we struck that day was for five years. The understanding amongst all at the meeting was that I had five years to find a rich husband as a long-term fix for the situation."

"Oh," Mrs. H said.

"Oh," I repeated. "Exactly. I think it was Mom's idea for me to come here, but it could have been the Order's as much as hers. I don't even know. I don't know if they're trying to control Emmett because they think they could control him if they gave him a wife like me—who theoretically will play by their rules. Or maybe they didn't think I'd cut it and thought we'd both fail out."

I flopped on my back on the bed. "I don't know anything! I just know I've never been able to live for myself or do what *I* want. Except within these walls. When I'm with Emmett, for the first time in forever, I feel like I'm truly just me. Like all the other voices in my head telling me to be perfect because it's what everyone expects finally shut the hell up, and I can just be... *me*."

"Well, dearie, why are ya tellin' all this to me? I expect

there's a hurting lad who needs to hear it much more than I do."

I grabbed for the pillow and yanked it over my face. Mrs. H yanked it away, glaring down at me.

"I can't!" I said, sitting up. "I don't know how! Emmett is the only person to look beneath all my masks and still like what he sees there. But I've been so terrified to peel back this last layer that proves I'm not his equal. He can't love someone who's not his equal; he's said it over and over—he can't trust them. He can't trust *me*." My voice cracked on the last word.

"But no matter how many times I wracked my brain, if I don't come out of this with a husband...." I looked up at Mrs. H with tear-soaked eyes. "Mom was so much better before I left, talking about all the things we'd do once I got back. She looked hopeful and almost like her old self. I couldn't bear to tell her that I wasn't sure if I could play the part of a cold-hearted gold-digger. But then I got here, and it was nothing like that. Emmett was nothing like.... He's amazing, Mrs. H. Beyond anything I could imagine. He's kind and gentle and caring but also dominant as hell. I can barely breathe when I'm around him; he makes me high. Not to mention the sex."

"Oh, I can imagine." She laughed, a giddy little giggle in her voice. "The walls aren't that thick."

"Mrs. H!" I giggled along with her, a little scandalized at knowing she could hear us.

But she just waved a hand. "It's healthy. Young folks have to get to know one another in all the important ways to find out if they're... ahem... compatible."

"Oh, we're compatible," I said, almost laughing, because we were so *intensely* compatible. "That's not the problem." I sighed.

"So what is, then, dearie?"

I just blinked at her. Hadn't she been listening to a word I said? "Everything else! He'll never forgive me. He'll never trust me! He'll never trust that I could love him for *him*—"

"And do you?" she cut me off.

I blanched at her just asking it outright. This was never supposed to be about love. But in the end, there was nothing to do but admit this final truth.

I nodded. "I never—"

But I wasn't able to finish my sentence, because right then, the door pushed in. It was Emmett, an unreadable expression on his face. My head jerked between him and the door. Wait, how long had he been there? Had he heard what we'd been talking about? Had he heard Mrs. H ask if I loved him? I hadn't been able to answer though, and he wouldn't have seen my nod.

I looked back at his face, determined to find some clue there, but his expression was stony as he met my gaze.

"They've called a Trial for tonight. It's our last one. If we pass, then we can finally be done with all this."

18

EMMETT

It was the last Trial.

And I wasn't sure what I was going to do. I'd disappeared again from the room this morning as soon as I saw her tear-stained face. She looked like hell, and she was also the most beautiful creature I'd ever seen. I couldn't get out of there fast enough. Knowing tonight would be the end of it was the only thing that kept me on the grounds at all today.

I'd never been a man to fail at anything. I gave my all with everything I did, and it'd always been good enough to succeed. The idea of throwing anything nearly makes me ill. But after the bomb of information that was just placed in my lap, I was actually considering failing the Initiation in the final hour. On purpose.

Bellamy and I walked up to the closed doors leading to the ballroom, both in complete silence. We had said all that needed to be said. I sure as fuck had anyway. She'd tried to start up again with, "Just hear me out before we go down," but I hadn't even looked her way. I'd simply started down the stairs, and after a couple of moments, she hurried to catch up.

I didn't even want to look at the girl, let alone be standing side by side with her, about to engage in a Trial that no doubt would involve me touching her, possibly even fucking her.

Which I didn't want to do.

My walls were up, my heart now safely secured, and the last thing I needed to do was fire missiles at it.

The only item in the box that arrived for tonight was a tux for me and a white satin robe for Bellamy. Doubtful she'd be wearing the robe for long; I tried my best to not picture it sliding off her shoulders. We both had no idea what was in store for the night, but considering it was the final Trial, we knew it wouldn't be easy to complete... if I even wanted to complete it.

The sound of footsteps approaching had us turning to see Mrs. H.

"Bellamy, you are to come with me to get ready for tonight." The woman's face showed no emotion or even a hint of what was to come. She'd been doing this for years and knew exactly how to conceal even the slightest hint if she chose. "Emmett, you're to go into the Billiards Room, where your friends are waiting for you."

Grateful to leave Bellamy and to have some time to gather my senses and some breathing space, I headed in the direction of the Billiards Room without saying another word or asking a single question.

As I entered, four men sitting around a circular table turned to look my way. Montgomery, Rafe, Walker, and Beau sat beneath a large Baccarat crystal-and-brass chandelier hanging from the fifteen-foot-high ceiling. Along the ceiling were plaster frieze moldings that were made from mud, clay, horsehair, and Spanish moss. I knew this room, as I had many a drink and cigar here. But this time felt different.

Beau Radcliffe was the first to speak casually as he sipped from his tumbler of scotch. "We've been beckoned to attend your final Trial tonight."

I turned to Walker, who hadn't completed his Initiation yet and wasn't a member of the Order. "Even you?"

Walker shrugged. "I got the invite. Not sure why."

I took my seat at the round table made of Honduran mahogany and reached for the bottle of scotch in the center of the table. "Do any of you have an idea of what's coming?"

Montgomery laughed. "It's been kept secret from your friends. Which is... odd."

Taking a sip of my drink, I leaned back and sighed. For the first time since Bellamy's *truth*, I felt like I could relax a little and be frank with my friends. "I don't think I'm going to become a member of the Order."

Beau huffed. "Don't worry about the final Trial. You'll do fine."

"Yeah, it's not going to be any harder than what you've already gone through," Montgomery added.

"It's not about the actual Trial," I began. "It's about Bellamy."

Every one of my friends, other than Walker, gave each other a knowing look.

Walker noticed and asked, "What did I miss?"

"Bellamy is flat-broke," Rafe answered. "It came out last night in front of everyone."

Walker shrugged. "No real secret there. People have been whispering about it for years."

"Bullshit," I snapped, not liking that this was information floating around Darlington. I didn't like being in the dark, but I also felt... sorry for... Bellamy if indeed people knew her deepest secret. "I haven't heard a single thing about her having money problems."

"It's true, man," Walker continued. "I know her mother came to my father and asked for money. Countless times. I know he helped when it suited him, but... he made the poor woman beg."

"Your dad's a dick," Montgomery mumbled more to himself than anyone else.

"And why do you care if Bellamy is broke or not?" Walker asked, ignoring Montgomery's insult.

"I don't," I said, drinking the rest of my scotch from my glass and pouring myself another. "I care that she lied to me, for one. And I also care about what her final ask is. The girl is expecting me to marry her if we complete the Initiation. She's asking for marriage!"

Walker let out a large exhale and then shook his head with a chuckle. "Man-oh-man."

"Yeah, so if I complete the final Trial, guess who gets a ring on her finger?" I prompted with a shake of my own head. "The fucked-up thing in all of this is... I actually liked Bellamy. I cared for her." I looked at the men around the table and confessed, "I was falling in love with her."

"Jesus," Montgomery said with an upturn of his lips. "I mean... you always had a thing for her."

"I did," I admitted. "And being locked up with the woman only added to my feelings. But it was all a lie. She's been lying to me from day one. She wants me for money, and that's it. She's no different than every other socialite out there, looking for a payday."

"I disagree. This is Bellamy Carmichael," Walker said calmly. "We've known her as long as we've known each other. There's more to her than what you want to admit, and we all know it. The girl had it rough. Her mother is a sociopath if you ask me. And her dad was a loser. But Bellamy... she's a cool chick."

"And you're lying to yourself right now," Rafe added.

Montgomery nodded. "I've watched you in these Trials with her. You've taken ownership in not only her body, but—"

"She's yours," Beau cut in. "It's obvious how you both feel for each other. She isn't just using you for your money. Even if that was her initial intent... it's clear in the way she looks at you, acts around you, and... it's obvious there is a deep connection between the two of you."

Giving a sardonic laugh, I closed my eyes briefly before asking, "So, I'm just supposed to complete whatever Trial is coming, allow her to get her wish, and marry her? Are you guys suggesting that? It's absurd."

"We don't know what the Elders will decide," Montgomery said. "But I'm suggesting that you finish what you started. Become a member of the Order like you've always wanted to do. Let fate take it from there."

"Even if fate means I get *married*?"

"You aren't one to quit," Walker added. "I know I haven't completed my own Initiation yet, and I have no idea just how difficult the Trials are, but I know if I just spent 109 days here, I sure as fuck wouldn't throw in the towel in the final hour."

"I wouldn't be the first person in our group to fail," I said softly, hating the idea of joining the ranks of outcasts but knowing it was a possibility.

"Sully failed... but he's a different story. He never wanted this. You do. You've wanted to be a member of The Order of the Silver Ghost maybe more than all of us. I know how important this is to you," Montgomery pointed out.

I hated that they were all right. I didn't want to fail. I wanted to be a member of the Order and had since I was a kid. "I just wish she hadn't lied to me."

"She's had to lie for years," Walker said. "I don't think she knows how to be truthful anymore in regard to her situation. And I can't say I blame her. Cut the poor girl some slack. None of us would want to admit what she's had to go through. And there isn't a man at this table who doesn't have secrets. Just because she withheld her past from you, doesn't mean she's a bad person."

"Says a man who isn't faced with marrying her," I bit out between clenched teeth. "And I never said she was a bad person."

Bellamy was far from a bad person. Yes, I was pissed. Furious with her. But the truth of the matter was my heart broke for her. If she had been honest with me and came to me for help, I would have given her every last cent needed. I would have... I would have never made her complete all these Trials, just so she could pay her bills.

I think that was where my real anger was.

I wanted to help Bellamy. I would have helped in every way.

I just didn't want to be tricked into doing it.

"Put the marriage idea aside for a second," Montgomery said as he reached for my empty glass and placed it next to him. Always the friend looking out for his buddies. I could see he didn't want me drinking anymore and drunk for tonight's Trial. "Do you care about Bellamy?"

I didn't want to answer the question. Not just to them, but I didn't want to face my truth to myself.

They all waited for my answer, and I could see there was no way I was getting out of this with just silence.

I sighed. "You all know I do. I always have."

"Then do what's right for the both of you. Complete this Trial. Get what you want, and allow her to get what she wants," Montgomery said.

"What she wants is marriage!"

"What she wants is security," he replied softly. "She wants to feel safe and secure for the first time in years. If you care about her like you say you do, then give her that. Marriage or not, she needs to complete this Initiation, or she walks away with nothing."

"Actually, she'd walk away in worse shape than arriving," Walker pointed out. "Now, everyone knows her secret. There's no hiding her financial situation from Darlington. She and her mother will be ruined in the world they both know and have lived. You need to at least give her something. Allow the Elders to at least compensate her."

"Fine," I said. "I'll complete the Trial. But if her final ask is marriage... you fuckers can't expect that from me."

"Just complete the Trial and then take it from there once the Initiation is behind you," Beau said.

An empty bottle of scotch and a half hour later of lectures and advice, the sound of a pistol being shot out in the garden finally announced our night was about to begin.

A man in a silver cloak arrived from a secret panel in the wall. The Elder motioned for us to follow him. And in total and complete silence, we obediently followed in single file down a narrow hallway leading us to the white ballroom.

Deep male voices chanted in Latin as we entered the room that had hundreds of white oleanders in tall crystal vases scattered around. The floral fragrance almost concealed the underlying feeling of doom that was to come. Oh so appropriate. The beautiful flowers' milky sap was poisonous, deadly so. The rhythmic beat of the canes rapping the floor reverberated through my bones.

"Emmett Washington," one of the Elders boomed. The

canes continued to beat. "Are you prepared to complete The Trials of Initiation?"

The canes increased in tempo.

Louder.

Louder.

Wind blew in from the open windows, swirling around us as if the Order had summoned the devil himself.

The Latin chanting began again as the gas lighting of the room flickered.

Then the sound of an organ mastered all other sounds. The song of the "Wedding March" began, and Bellamy, completely naked, walked through the double doors.

"Emmett Washington. Your final Trial of Initiation shall begin."

19

BELLAMY

They had me up on an elevated platform they set up in the center of the room when Emmett walked in.

I could barely make out the expression on his face—blank, monotone—before the lights in the room dimmed, all but for the spotlights at the bottom of the platform shining on me. The beaming lights blinded me to the dark room beyond my platform and its sphere of illumination. I squinted to try to make out Emmett, but he effectively disappeared into the dark crowd.

If only I had a few minutes to talk to him before we'd been dragged into yet another Trial. I tried, but he denied me, first by staying away from the room all day and then again by not letting me get in two words before heading downstairs.

After all the weeks of interminable waiting, now everything was going too fast. If only it would all slow down. If I could just call a time-out so I could grab Emmett and talk to him on the sidelines....

But no—I was standing up here on this platform in the

center of the room, and Mr. St. Claire was standing beside me with an auctioneer's block in front of him.

He pounded a gavel on it several times. "Quiet, quiet, the auction is now beginning. Tonight, we'll be auctioning off the favors of the delectable Ms. Bellamy Carmichael. To the highest bidder go the spoils!"

He banged the gavel several more times and then began to speak in that quick-tongued auctioneer speech I'd heard one painful time when I let myself be dragged to a rodeo; once was enough—trust me.

He banged the gavel several more times and then spoke loudly, "For the honor of kissing, fondling, and finger-fucking, we'll start the bidding off at $1,000. Do I hear $1,000?"

He pointed out at the crowd. "One thousand, do I hear two? Two thousand." He pointed in a different direction. They'd arranged lights at the bottom of the podium blaring up at me, and I couldn't tell man from man as hands with paddles lifted all throughout the room. I shrank back and lifted my arm over my eyes.

Emmett had come in from the back center though, so I squinted that direction. Was he bidding on me? Was he even still in the room?

"Ten thousand," said a loud, firm voice from the back of the room, and my heart leapt. Emmett. There was no mistaking that baritone.

My cheeks flamed as I stared out into the dark crowd where his voice had come from. They couldn't have thought up a crueler challenge. Here I was, literally forcing him to spend his money on me. To buy my love.

Or at least my body.

Maybe that was it—maybe this was for me. To show me what I really was. What I always was. Just a whore he had to pay for.

"Twenty-five thousand. Do I have—"

"Seventy thousand," called a man's voice from the left.

"Eighty thousand," said another, nearer.

"A million dollars and we're done," Emmett said as he stormed to the front of the room.

I trembled, and not just because I was standing naked in a chilly room surrounded by thirty men. A *million* dollars?

"By all means," said the auctioneer to Emmett, moving away and holding out a hand in invitation toward me, the prize. "Enjoy your winnings before we move on to auctioning off her other... charms. So many heavy pockets here tonight, ready to spend."

Emmett's jaw tensed, and from the flash in his eye as he took the large step up onto the platform, I was afraid for a moment he might deck the auctioneer. Mr. St. Claire was the most important Elder and the man that, previous to now, Emmett had wanted most to impress.

Was he mad about spending the money? Why had he done it? Was it just a point of pride for him at this point that no one else would touch me? He had to maintain face in front of these men, after all.

It was the only reason I could imagine he'd do it. I ruined everything else between us.

I had no more pride though, and I was determined to say what I'd been too much of a coward to say before. If I couldn't have my time-out, right here right now would have to do.

So as Emmett stood in front of me, blocking out the light from the spotlights as Mr. St. Claire took the three stairs off the platform at the back, I took my chance.

"Emmett," I said, my voice trembling, "I'm sorry. I'm sorry for all of it. I never meant for...." Then I shook my head, angry at myself for wasting words when there was no time. "I love you. I fell in love with you. I'm sorry for everything else, but I'll never be sorry for that."

Emmett's nostrils flared, and his eyes burned. Was I finally getting through to him?

But his hand came from nowhere, lashing out and grabbing me around the throat. I barely managed to suck in a breath before he started squeezing. "Bend over the auction block."

I nodded, breath trapped in my chest. He squeezed tighter, and I got the message.

I was no longer in control. I no longer had any say in how this was going to go.

I lowered my eyes, nodded as much as I could with his thick fingers wrapped around my neck, and submitted.

I moved to the auctioneer's block. It was a thick butcher's block more than a podium. I braced my hands against it and bent over, assuming the position.

"Count," he said, his voice like a whip. "And beg me for more."

And then he began to spank me in front of the whole room. With each *smack* upward from the underside of my ass, my cheeks jiggled obscenely.

"Two, may I have another, Sir? Three, may I have anoth — Four!"

I danced on my toes at that, an especially hard one. "May I have another, Sir?" I barely managed to get out through my teeth.

Then came five and six, leaving me breathless as I asked for more.

Right when I thought I was finally easing into the swing of things, suddenly Emmett's thick finger was pushing between my legs, demanding entrance.

He slid easily into my secret place, because... I was wet. The second his hand made contact with my skin, my body had started priming for him. He'd trained me well over the last three months.

And the truth was, being up here on display for everyone like this, even in these fucked-up circumstances... I couldn't help it. I was still turned on. This was who I was, at least when it was Emmett's hands on my body. It was who he'd made me, who we became together.

So when he started to finger-fuck me relentlessly, first with one finger, and then two, all I could do was widen my stance and open to him so he had better access.

I felt the weight of him move against my back, and then he pulled his fingers out of me. But only so he could shove them in my mouth. "Taste how wet you are for my touch. Clean yourself off my fucking fingers."

I suckled urgently at his thick fingers in my mouth, and I felt him harden through his slacks against my ass. I sucked even harder, until he made me gasp by twisting my nipple *hard* with his free hand. He pulled his fingers out of my mouth with my gasp, then he had both of my heavy breasts in his hands.

And he was not gentle. He punished my nipples, plucking and twisting them until I cried out. Oh, he seemed to like that, because he kept going, shoving one of his knees between my legs as he continued, squeezing my nipples so hard, pinching each of them ruthlessly between his fingers. He shoved upward with his knee at the same time, twisting and pinching. My eyes went wide, my mouth dropping open in agonizing pleasure.

And then all of a sudden, he let go, shoving even harder against my groin with his knee—and I came. And I came and came, until he yanked his knee away, and I was left wet and gasping, barely satisfied as I sagged against the auction block.

"What a sweet little hair-trigger you've got trained there," Mr. St. Claire said, hopping back up on the platform as Emmett stepped even farther away. I wanted to reach for him, but he was jumping off the podium, and then he was gone into the darkness beyond the spotlights. I was left heaving and bereft.

He'd never left me so coldly after making me come. He was usually so good with after-care. He always made sure I was okay, that I was stable and taken care of.

But everything was different now. It would never be like that again. I tried to fight against the tears that slid down my cheeks but to no avail.

Was this his plan? Did Emmett just want to decimate me completely in this—our last time ever together?

It was too late for me. I'd submitted. I'd go wherever my master wanted to take me tonight. Descend to whatever depths he wanted to take me. Pay any penance.

"I think we're all eager to get our hands on this sweet little whimpering piece of ass after that demonstration. Who wants to feel those sweet lips sucking your cock as eagerly as she just sucked Initiate Emmett's fingers? Because that's what's up for auction next. How much to empty your load into Ms. Carmichael's sweet mouth? Bidding starts at fifty thousand. Fifty thousand, do I hear fifty—?"

"Fifty," said someone.

"I've got fifty, and I want seventy-five. Do I hear seventy-five? Seventy-five, looking for seventy-five—"

"Two hundred thousand," said a voice from the left.

"Two hundred thousand, do I have three? Three hundred thousand, would you go to three hundred—"

"A million," came Emmett's voice again.

Jesus, again?

But the auctioneer just took it in stride. "A million. Do I have a million and a quarter? A million and a quarter? A million and a quarter? I've got a million, looking for a million and a quarter."

The room stayed silent, and again, Emmett strode forward. He wasn't empty-handed though. I didn't know where he'd gotten it, but he was holding a bundle of red silk rope.

My eyes shot to his, but he wasn't looking at me.

"Kneel," was all he said, a cold order barked in my direction. I immediately dropped to the floor. In for a penny, in for a pound. In spite of how wrong things were between us, submission required trust, and I trusted him. I meant what I said. I loved him, and love inherently included trust. I could only demonstrate my truth through my actions.

So I knelt, and when he moved behind me, pulled one arm behind my back, and began looping rope around my arms, tying my wrist to my ankle, I didn't make a single peep of protest.

Only when he finally had me the way he wanted me, trussed up until I could barely move, on my knees with my arms tied to my ankles, did he finally go to stand in front of me and look down at me.

I looked up at him, and our eyes caught for a moment, just a moment, before his hands were on the button and zipper of his pants. He pulled himself out, and my eyes widened. He was engorged—huge and what had to be almost painfully hard. Good Lord, how long had he been like that? The entire time he was tying me up?

I licked my lips and then looked up at him.

He bent down so that his head was beside mine. "The

act of snapping is your safe word. But only use it if you mean it. Because I'm not going to take it easy on you. Nod if you understand."

He pulled back, and I looked up at him, swallowing hard as I nodded. My back was arched, and my breasts thrust out the way he'd tied me. It was far from comfortable, but when I glanced down at myself, I had to admit it was an incredibly erotic sight.

But I had only a moment to look, because the next second, Emmett was grabbing me beneath the chin and then shoving his fat cock between my lips.

Murmurs went through the crowd as he began to fuck my face. There were no other words for what he was doing. He was using me. Using me like one might a sex doll. It was degrading. Humiliating.

And I was so turned on.

Perfect cotillion Darlington daughter, on my knees while the strongest, most powerful man in the room had me tied up, fucking my face. He grabbed the back of my hair and bottomed out, his cock going down my throat until I choked a little on him. He growled, and I could tell he liked that. So did the other men in the room.

So I closed my lips around him and sucked with as much vacuum pressure as I could manage until Emmett groaned and pulled back. I pulled in a breath before he thrust back in.

I wished I had my hands free so I could fondle his balls, making it even better for him.

When he next pulled out, I yanked free of his grasp on my hair, ignoring a few hairs pulled free, and ducked to suck one of his balls into my mouth. He gasped as I laved it with my tongue and then moved on to the other.

He growled but let me play—at least for a few seconds

more—before grabbing my face again with both of his hands and bringing his stiffer-than-ever cock to my lips. He bobbed the full-to-bursting crown in and out of my mouth. I suckled the tip, licking right up the slit and then covering the crown with my mouth, pressing hard with my tongue on the vein underneath the tip.

That sent him crazy again. He clutched my head harder and pushed in and out, in and out.

"Paint her lips, Initiate," called a voice from the crowd.

He pulled his cock out, so thick his hand barely fit around the girth of it, and looked me in the eye as he used the tip like a paintbrush to cover my lips in the precum leaking out of his cock. My chest arched out even more toward him. I never would've thought a blowjob could turn me on this much, but everything concerning Emmett did —and God, seeing him hold his magnificent cock like that....

I licked the lips he'd just coated with himself, and apparently, that was the final straw. He shoved himself in to the root, his balls slapping my chin.

And he unloaded down my throat.

I swallowed convulsively. Swallow after swallow of him. But he dragged himself out while he was still coming, so his cum dribbled onto my chin and down my chest.

The crowd around us roared as he rubbed himself all over me, claiming and marking me in the most primitive way possible.

Then, as before, as soon as he was done, he zipped himself back up. I barely even saw him whip out a pocket knife. The ropes binding my wrists to my ankles were slashed, and I was released. But when I turned to look behind me, Emmett was already gone, back into the crowd.

I swallowed hard, his essence still salty on my tongue,

blinking and feeling overwhelmed by all that was happening. But I would hold strong.

Because there was at least still one more part of me to be auctioned off.

My pussy went for ten million dollars.

Again to Emmett.

There was a moment when the auctioneer had paused at two million when I thought Emmett would bow out, but then he came in with that astounding number.

Tonight, he spent twelve million dollars on me. Money that went to the Order, I supposed. Money that was pocket change to Emmett but would have been life changing for me. I still had no clue what was going to come of all of this, but by the time Emmett climbed back up on the platform and told me to lie down with my arms and legs spread, I couldn't care.

Master was here, and that was all that mattered in this moment.

He stood tall as he towered over my prone and spread-out body. He wasn't looking at me; his eyes were out on the crowd.

"I want to call on my brothers to assist me. Montgomery. Beau. Rafe. Walker. Come here. Each of you, hold down one of her limbs. Grab an ankle or wrist. Hold her still while I claim my ten-million-dollar prize."

I felt my face flame as murmurs went through the crowd. I lifted my head just the littlest bit and saw movement around the room. Oh my God, was he serious? He was going to have our old school friends lay hands on me while he... while he fucked me?

This was taking voyeurism to the next level.

But apparently none of the men complained, because one by one, I felt a manly hand clamp around each of my appendages. It was my left ankle first. Then my right. Then a hand grabbed my wrist. I looked up, and pure embarrassment flashed through me to see Walker St. Claire holding one wrist and Montgomery Kingston taking the other.

Montgomery held my wrist but averted his eyes. Walker didn't bother. He glanced down at me and grinned, only looking away when Emmett approached. Emmett pulled his dress shirt off over his head and threw it to the ground beyond the podium. But he didn't remove his pants, just unbuttoned them again and shoved them down past his ass.

And somehow, he was fully erect again. He was the only man I'd ever been with who could accomplish this. It had only been maybe ten minutes since he'd last come, and yet here he was again, hard as ever.

"How does it feel, little girl, to have other men's hands on you while I fuck you?" he whispered in my ear as he eased his body over mine. "Be honest now."

I sucked in a breath. "Strange. But n-not bad. I only want you inside me though."

He didn't waste time. After all the other pageantry of the evening, he just grabbed his cock and guided it inside me.

He looked down and to both sides. "Hold her open for me. A little wider."

The hands holding my ankles adjusted, stretching me wider. I gasped as Emmett's hips slid in a little closer, his cock notching that much deeper inside me.

"Pull those legs wide. Up toward her head."

The hands holding my ankles did, manhandling me while Emmett held himself up with his strong biceps and pumped into me.

"Anyone else who wants can take turns holding my pet down," Emmett said to the crowd at large. "But hands only. I'm the only cock fucking her."

My eyes widened, and Emmett smiled down at me. And the thing was, I didn't think he was doing this for revenge. Yeah, he might still be pissed at me, and maybe this was a test... but he also still really got off on this.

He was one kinky motherfucker, and this right here, having an entire room at his command while getting to show off his prowess over me—this was Emmett as he was always meant to be. Commanding. In control.

And I wanted him more than ever. He broke all the rules I'd been raised with my whole life—always do what's expected of you; never make waves. No, he took these dirty old fucks and bested them at their own games. He was one-upping them, showing them that we could play dirty, filthy, erotic games without hurting anyone. He was the richest and the most powerful of them all, and he was here to teach them a lesson instead of meekly accepting whatever they'd been trying to prove with this Trial. But he was still inviting them in to play with him.

I felt my heart open up even more as Emmett's cock lit up every single one of my pleasure centers with each thrust.

My limbs were handed off. Other hands took possession of my legs, and the new handlers weren't as reticent as our high school friends. The new hands took liberties. They caressed my legs and arms. Teasing fingers pinched occasionally.

But they obeyed Emmett. No one shoved a cock in my face or tried to put anything in my ass. Ha, as if they could have gotten in between me and Emmett's huge body towering over me.

"Close your eyes," Emmett barked at me. "Feel us. Don't think. Feel our hands. They are all my hands. Feel my cock. I want them to feel you shake as you come over and over again. I want them to feel what I do to you."

"May I come, Master?" I begged.

"Not yet," he said, his hips pulling back and then slamming into me, his balls slapping my ass. God, I loved that filthy sound and the pressure of him when he hit my cervix like that. As he dragged out, his bulbous head hit my G-spot. The more he fucked me, the harder it was to hold back.

I mewled and flexed against all the hands holding me down so that they really had to work to keep me from reaching for Emmett.

"Please, please," I pleaded only a minute later. "Please, may I come?"

"I don't know if you're ready yet," Emmett said. "Someone, pinch her nipples."

Greedy hands came to my breasts. Emmett looked in my eyes as hands, hands everywhere, grasped at me—massaging, pinching, rubbing my ass, along my flanks.

I was seconds from popping off. My fingers flexed and clenched. "May I come, Sir?" I cried, desperate.

"Come," Emmett demanded, dropping his body lower against mine so that his groin ground down against my clit as he dragged his thick cock out and in.

Fireworks lit behind my eyelids as my orgasm exploded outward from my sex. My legs shook with the power of it, so intense not even all the hands on me could keep me still.

Emmett kept fucking me through it, so goddamned glorious, and it was one of the most intense experiences of my life.

Especially because, knowing my talents for multiple orgasms from our time together in the room, he immediately demanded, "Ride it into another one, higher this time. Harder. Fucking harder. *Come!*"

I did. Lord, did I come. The first one had just been an appetizer, but now we were on to the main entree as I lost words. Lost thought. Pleasure. Body-quaking, soul-shaking pleasure.

The hands on me squeezed, massaging harder than ever as the spasms ran through my body. So erotic, all of them surrounding me.

So many hands, all at Emmett's command.

My belly spasmed as a fresh orgasm started. Emmett held himself up with one arm as he reached down and grabbed my ass roughly, gripping me half by my hip, half by my ass as he dragged me up and down his cock, all the rest of the men helping with the motion, until Emmett sat up and the men pulled me with him.

They were lifting me up and down his cock. More men than I could count now climbed up on the platform. Some had their cocks out, one hand on me, the other jacking themselves. Others were fully engaged in holding me up and helping me fuck Emmett, still interested in caressing newly exposed parts of me—my back, down to the curve of my ass.

I was a puppet, and they held all my strings.

Until it was Emmett lying down, and they held me as I rode him. Emmett's hands were on my hips, guiding my motion. But otherwise, other men held onto almost every inch of me.

"Come," Emmett demanded again.

Oh my God, he was going to kill me. We felt like one giant, gyrating sex organism up on this platform, all moving in tandem for one goal.

Of course I came. I couldn't have stopped it, as sensitized as I was now, for all the world. I'd already been riding so high it was nothing to trip back into another orgasm.

I threw my head back and screamed as hands grasped

my breasts and yanked my hair, and all around me, men furiously yanked on their cocks, lust heavy in the air.

As I squeezed convulsively on Emmett's cock, he roared and thrust deep. I felt the jettison of his cum deep inside me, but then he quickly pulled out, even as more cum dripped out. He painted my pussy with the rest of his cum until I was a sweaty, sticky mess.

But he wasn't done—no, not nearly done. He looked around us. "I'm a giving man. So any man who's shared in my prize may come now if they wish, but only at her feet."

No one batted an eye. Maybe they were humoring him, or maybe they'd all been captured by Emmett's commanding nature as much as I had. Maybe it was simply a new game, and these bastards were always up for new and kinky.

Either way, Emmett helped me to my feet and stood behind me, hands plucking my breasts as man after man came to the side of the platform and masturbated at my feet. Men's cum splashed my feet and shins as they worshipped at the shrine of *me*.

Until finally, all were spent.

I expected that to be the end of it, and apparently so did Emmett, because he took my arm, ostensibly to lead me from the makeshift stage, when Mr. St. Claire took the steps.

I'd just seen him red-faced and sweaty as he jacked off his midsized cock at my feet, but he had his silver Elder's robe back on and a smile on his face.

"Where are you going, Initiate? We have one last item to auction off."

"What's left?" Emmett growled. "We gave you everything you wanted and more."

Emmett was truly pissed; I could tell, even though he

was still standing partially behind me. I wanted to cower and cover myself. The high of the kinky sex was wearing off, and Emmett's angry voice was a dash of cold reality over the endorphins I'd been feeling.

"The most important item, of course. The last item to be auctioned off is Bellamy Carmichael's hand in marriage."

20

EMMETT

"**A**nother ten million and this Trial is over," I said between clenched teeth.

If any man dared to even mention a bid for Bellamy, my wrath and delicate revenge would be swift. I had few enemies in life, but I wouldn't hesitate to take on a roomful if need be.

Bellamy Carmichael would not belong to another soul. Not while I was on this earth.

I would double the money if I had to, but if any man had the nerve to even *try* to take her from me....

It wasn't about the money. I had it, and I'd make what I spent tonight quickly. It was the fact that I was sick of The Order of the Silver Ghost and their twisted games. I couldn't leave the Oleander fast enough and seriously questioned if I'd ever return—member or not. I was over trying to impress these men.

Why the fuck did I even bother or care?

I didn't need their approval, and for some insane reason, I had wanted it.

But tonight wasn't about them. It wasn't about impressing the Elders.

No... it was about Bellamy Carmichael.

I could act as pissed off as I wanted. I could say I didn't give a shit about her. I could threaten to walk away and screw up everything for not only me but her. I could destroy her life and detonate a bomb that would cause her to have to walk out of this manor empty-handed. And if I hadn't outbid all the fuckers in this room earlier, I could have allowed her to become used up goods by every powerful man in Darlington County.

But apparently, it had taken this Trial to prove it to myself. My friends couldn't talk me into it. It was seeing Bellamy up there, naked, gorgeous, and in need of me. Maybe it made me as much a fool as I'd been in high school, but I didn't think so.

When she whispered in my ear that she loved me, I believed her. And more than that, I was ready to prove to her I was no coward. I was ready to take the leap of trust and love, whether or not she'd be there to meet me on the other side.

That was what a real *man* did.

I had to protect her, and there wasn't any amount of money I wouldn't spend to do so.

She was mine, and it was damn time that I showed not only her but every man who stood around us.

"Ten million for Bellamy Carmichael's hand in marriage," Elder St. Claire said. "Are there any other bids?"

Momentary silence filled the room, and I took the opportunity to stare into Bellamy's wide eyes that locked with mine. I couldn't read her and wished I could. Was she angry with me for what just occurred? Relieved it was me she'd be marrying? Surprised I agreed after how I treated her?

"Very well," Mr. St. Claire said. "Her hand now belongs to you. You have 109 days from this day to be engaged, make arrangements for a wedding, and recite your vows on the grounds of the Oleander. Do I have your word, Emmett, that you will follow through?"

I nodded. "You have my word. We will be married within 109 days."

The canes banged on the floor in a cadence that vibrated throughout my entire core.

"Emmett Washington, Bellamy Carmichael, you have both passed the Initiation. Emmett, you are now a member of The Order of the Silver Ghost. Bellamy, you have been granted your wish and have Emmett as your future husband." He pounded his cane hard to punctuate his dictate.

Removing my jacket, I placed it over Bellamy's shoulders and noticed she was trembling. Hating that she had to stand in the ballroom so exposed, especially after such an intense sexual experience, I chastised myself for not doing it sooner. Pulling her body into mine to offer some heat, I released a deep breath that I hadn't even realized I was holding.

Not waiting for any more to be said, I escorted her out of the ballroom and back to our room as a million thoughts ran through my head. But just like approaching difficult situations in business, I knew I had to treat this the same way.

One step at a time.

Right now, I needed to get Bellamy warmed up and out of this den of vipers.

When we reached our room, she instantly looked up at me, still keeping her body pressed against mine. "You don't have to marry me. It's not fair that I put those terms as my ask. I won't hold you to it. I'm so sorry I ever did."

"The Elders will make sure of it," I said and noticed how her body tensed. "And besides, when I make a commitment, I keep it. I told them we would be married in the time frame, and I plan to be a man of my word."

She lowered her eyes to the floor as I led her to the bathroom to get her in the shower to cleanse this night away. "I'm sorry. I know I asked for marriage, and... I wasn't thinking. I was allowing my mother to do the thinking for me. I never meant to trap you." When the water was warm enough, she stepped in and breathed out, "Once we're married and you have honored your word, we can always get the marriage annulled if you want. I won't expect you to remain married to me." Her eyes were downcast. "I understand why you'd want to end it."

"I never said I'd want to end it."

Her eyes flashed up in surprise. "But you deserve better! You didn't go into this Initiation intending to get married. It's not what you bargained for," she said.

I perched myself on the edge of the sink, watching her run her hair beneath the stream of water. "Why didn't you tell me about your mother? About your father and your financial situation?" I asked, needing to hear why.

"I was ashamed," she stated simply. "You know how Darlington is."

"But I'm not Darlington."

She turned her head to look at me through the shower glass. "No. You most certainly aren't Darlington. But your opinion of me matters more than anything and over everyone else. So I hid everything to try to preserve that." She sighed. "And in the end, I made you hate me. You had every right to know the truth. My truth."

"I don't hate you," I confessed. "The opposite, in fact."

She turned off the water, and I handed her a towel. Her hand brushed mine, and I felt my body come alive again. "The opposite?" she asked, her voice quivering as she did.

"I love you, Bellamy." I took her into my arms and held her close, her body wet and steaming. "I've always loved you... since the first days in the high school lunchroom."

"I love you," she mumbled against my chest, wet hair soaking my shirt. I didn't care; having her in my arms was everything. "So much."

"I just wish I had known," I murmured into her hair. "I would have helped."

She shook her head, her face still against my chest. "I never would have asked that of you." She pulled her face away and looked up at me. "And I still won't. I know you are a man of your word, but it's not fair to expect you to marry me by force."

"It's not by force," I said, lowering my lips to her forehead and kissing her softly. "I would have never bid on your hand in marriage if I didn't intend to make good on it."

She groaned and pressed her face back into my chest. "It was so much money. You spent so much tonight... on me."

"And I'd do it again and again."

"Why?" Her voice was so fragile and nearly a whisper.

"Because *you* deserve it. You deserve to be protected, loved, and cared for. You deserve to know just how valuable you are." It all felt so easy to say, now that I let myself. And watching the disbelief and joy wage war on her face made it all worth it. But I'd make her believe, day and night for the rest of her life, if that was what it took.

Bellamy took a deep breath and took a step back from me. She held the towel tight around her, her wet hair dripping down her back, her makeup washed off, and I had never found her more beautiful than I did right then.

"So what now? What do we do now?" she asked.

"We leave the Oleander the moment you get dressed. We can't leave this place fast enough. And then we go home—to my home. What will soon be *our* home. And then in the morning, we sit down with your mother and figure out the finances. I plan to fix it and make everything right."

"I can't ask that of you," she whispered, still blinking in disbelief. "I know it was the plan when my mother and I first intended on me being a Belle, but—"

"It's an easy fix for me. And I want to do it. Not just because I can, or because I feel it's part of the deal of the Initiation, but because I want to. I genuinely want to. Your mother is going to be part of my family, and I take care of what is mine. And though I'm not happy with the fact that she put you in this situation, and I have some feelings on how she's treated you, she is still your mother and a woman who deserves the respect of Darlington. This is an easy fix."

I took her hand and led her to the bathroom and reached for my suitcase. She followed suit and began to dress.

"So what's a hard fix?" she asked, laughing like she could still hardly believe everything that was happening as she pulled a dress over her head. "You've mentioned *easy fix* a few times, which leads me to think there's a hard one."

"Yes, we have a few challenges ahead." I began packing, not wanting to be in this room another second longer than need be.

"You mean me? Living together?"

I laughed loudly. "I think we've proven we know how to live together." I gave her a wink before adding, "No, we have a very large challenge ahead of us, and I worry if we'll survive it."

She stopped and stared at me with concern all over her face. "What?"

I crossed the room and took her hands in mine. "We only have 109 days to plan a wedding, and I have a feeling that between you and your mother... well, I'm starting to worry you might be a Bridezilla."

Bellamy's entire face lit up as she laughed and shook her head. "I promise I won't— Okay... no promises. I may be. But I'll try to behave and keep my mother on a leash." She laughed again and flung her arms around my neck. "I don't know how I got so lucky to have you in my life, Emmett Washington."

"Because you chose to be a Belle," I said, stating the obvious. "And I was smart enough to choose you."

"I choose you back," she said as she lifted on tiptoe to kiss me.

"And I will continue to choose you. Over and over again."

Our lips met, and she was the sweetest nectar I'd ever tasted.

EPILOGUE
WALKER ST. CLAIRE

Having beers with the guys wasn't something we've been able to do in a while. With all of our Trials, life, and... well... it was nice to be sitting for a cold one with my friends again.

"I can't believe you're getting married in one week," I said to Emmett. "How does it feel?"

Emmett chuckled, took a sip of his beer, and then answered, "I feel relief. The wedding planning with my future mother-in-law is about as close to hell as I hope to get. I mean, I like the woman, but man-oh-man. This wedding has to be perfect in her eyes."

"Well, it's her only daughter," Montgomery said, "and it *is* Darlington County."

"I still can't believe y'all have either wifed up or are getting damn close," I said, surprised to see such a change in my friends' statuses in such a short time. "It's like the Oleander has become some wedding trap or something. What ever happened to the tradition of it being the house of debauchery and sin?"

"Oh, trust me," Rafe said with a huff. "It's all of that and more."

"Yeah, you just wait until it's your turn," Beau added. "You'll see."

"I still feel we need to make a change though," Montgomery said, his big smile fading to his normal serious expression. "Once we're all members—" He looks at me. "—and start grooming to become Elders, we need to change the old ways. They're fucked."

"You sound like Sully," I said. "And I'm more of a traditionalist. I don't think we have to modernize everything. Sometimes, we should just respect history."

"Sully's right," Montgomery said quickly. "And you haven't seen or been through what we have. You will soon enough, and I have a feeling you won't want to keep to tradition like you think."

"Well, it can't all be bad if y'all found the love of your lives during the Initiation." I shrugged and took another swallow of my beer. "My Initiation is going to be far different than yours, however. I can't marry a Belle. I can't even think of being with one at the end. Unlike you guys, I have to think about my reputation and how I'll come out looking when this is all done. I can't run for Mayor like I plan with a soiled reputation. And I can't risk my future wife having a past that is anything unsavory to the Darlington voters. Y'all know I have to care about lineage and name, and... it's politics."

My buddies all rolled their eyes but in good fun. They knew how important politics were to me. I had been groomed to follow the same path as my father since birth. It was who I was and my entire identity.

The Oleander, The Order of the Silver Ghost, and the Initiation were the final step to make that happen. I needed to become a member to get all the support and backing that was required to secure the votes to win.

"I sure as hell never thought I'd be planning a wedding when I was done with the Trials," Emmett said. "You'll see just how much you can't control your destiny once you're within those walls. The Oleander can be a real bitch that way. It's also not a given that you'll pass just because your father is an Elder. There's going to be a lot of Trials you won't want to do. And even your daddy can't help you."

I nodded in agreement, even though I didn't believe it. I truly felt that me going through the Trials was all a technicality and for show. I would be a member and, very soon after, become one of the Elders. I had been groomed for this too.

There was one big truth to being born and raised in Darlington.

Your book of life, and each chapter in it, had been written for you.

No rewrites allowed.

~

A MONTH AND A HALF LATER

"What do you mean she quit?" I stared, uncomprehending, into Mrs. H's sorrowful face.

"She came to me in the middle of the night and begged me not to wake you. She said she couldn't go on."

I scrambled out of bed and stared at the empty space beside me. Where my Belle was supposed to be.

The Belle who had apparently just quit on me.

"Did she say why?" I dragged my hands through my hair,

then reached for my pants. I was only wearing boxers but was too upset to be embarrassed about it in front of Mrs. H. Maybe if I went after the girl and tried to convince her to change her mind before anyone found out....

"The Elders know already. They're downstairs. They've called a conclave to decide what to do with you now."

Shit. I sat back down heavily on the bed and looked helplessly back up at Mrs. H. "What else did she *say*? I didn't think things were going that bad."

True, things between me and my Belle, Sarah, hadn't seemed to be going as magically as it had for all my best friends. They'd ended up with true love, and things with Sarah and me had been... well, fine. They'd been *fine*.

We hadn't even had any death-defying Trials or anything yet. And she hadn't balked at the tattoo. She seemed eager enough for the sex, and the rest of the time, all she wanted to do was watch TV.

Fine with me. I had work to do. I thought we had a good thing going, both of us getting what we wanted out of the deal.

But now, she'd up and left me holding the damn bag.

What the actual fuck?

"She didn't say anything else, and it doesn't matter now. You should hurry, love," Mrs. H said, worry lines in her forehead. "They're waiting. And your father doesn't look happy."

I swallowed and stood.

No rewrites. And now it was time to face whatever fate had in store for me. Because apparently, my future was suddenly very different from the one I'd always envisioned for myself.

Because no St. Claire heir had ever failed the Trials, not in six generations.

Until me.

~

The Breaking Belles series continues with the final book
Lavish Corruption
Are you ready for Walker St. Claire's story?
Coming in 2022

~

Want a **bonus scene** of a dark initiation ritual between
Grace and Montgomery, the main characters from Elegant
Sins? For some extra dark, extra sacrilegious sizzle, read the
scene that was too dark to make it into the book.
Go to BookHip.com/WPQXMJ to get it NOW!

ALSO BY STASIA BLACK

Love So Dark [https://geni.us/LoSDa-EN-w]

Theirs To Protect [https://geni.us/Th2Pr-EN-w]

Theirs To Pleasure [https://geni.us/Th2Pl-EN-w]

Theirs To Wed [https://geni.us/Th2We-EN-w]

Theirs To Defy [https://geni.us/Th2De-EN-w]

Theirs To Ransom [https://geni.us/Th2Ra-EN-w]

Marriage Raffle Boxset Part 1 [https://geni.us/MaRaBx-EN-w]

Marriage Raffle Boxset Part 2 [https://geni.us/MaRaBx-2-EN-w]

FREEBIE

Their Honeymoon [https://BookHip.com/QHCQDM]

ALSO BY ALTA HENSLEY

For all of my books, check out my Amazon Page!

http://amzn.to/2CTmeen

<u>Secret Bride Series:</u>

Captive Bride

Kept Bride

Taken Bride

<u>Top Shelf Series:</u>

Bastards & Whiskey

Villains & Vodka

Scoundrels & Scotch

Devils & Rye

Beasts & Bourbon

Sinners & Gin

<u>Evil Lies Series:</u>

The Truth About Cinder

The Truth About Alice

ABOUT STASIA BLACK

STASIA BLACK grew up in Texas, recently spent a freezing five-year stint in Minnesota, and now is happily planted in sunny California, which she will never, ever leave.

She loves writing, reading, listening to podcasts, and has recently taken up biking after a twenty-year sabbatical (and has the bumps and bruises to prove it). She lives with her own personal cheerleader, aka, her handsome husband, and their teenage son. Wow. Typing that makes her feel old. And writing about herself in the third person makes her feel a little like a nutjob, but ahem! Where were we?

Stasia's drawn to romantic stories that don't take the easy way out. She wants to see beneath people's veneer and poke into their dark places, their twisted motives, and their deepest desires. Basically, she wants to create characters that make readers alternately laugh, cry ugly tears, want to toss their kindles across the room, and then declare they have a new FBB (forever book boyfriend).

Join Stasia's Facebook Group for Readers for access to deleted scenes, to chat with me and other fans and also get access to exclusive giveaways:

Stasia's Facebook Reader Group

Want to read an EXCLUSIVE, FREE novella, Indecent: a Taboo Proposal, that is available ONLY to my newsletter subscribers, along with news about upcoming releases, sales, exclusive giveaways, and more?

Get **Indecent: a Taboo Proposal**

When Mia's boyfriend takes her out to her favorite restaurant on their six-year anniversary, she's expecting one kind of proposal. What she didn't expect was her boyfriend's longtime rival, Vaughn McBride, to show up and make a completely different sort of offer: all her boyfriend's debts will be wiped clear. The price?

One night with her.

～

ABOUT ALTA HENSLEY

Alta Hensley is a USA TODAY bestselling author of hot, dark and dirty romance. She is also an Amazon Top 100 bestselling author. Being a multi-published author in the romance genre, Alta is known for her dark, gritty alpha heroes, sometimes sweet love stories, hot eroticism, and engaging tales of the constant struggle between dominance and submission.

∼

As a gift for being my reader, I would like to offer you a FREE book.

DELICATE SCARS

∼

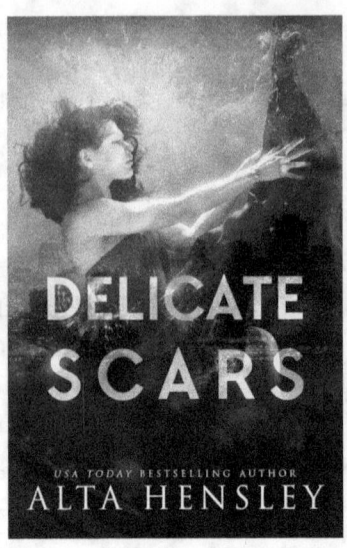

Get your copy now! ~
https://dl.bookfunnel.com/tnpuad5675

I was going to ruin her.

I knew it the moment I laid eyes on her. She was too naive, too innocent.

I would wrap her in the darkness of my world till she no longer craved the light... only me.

I should walk away, leave her clean and untouched... but I won't.

I hold her delicate heart in my scarred fist and I have no intention of letting go.

It all started with a book... doesn't that sound crazy?

For your entire world to come crashing down around you over research for a book?

But that is what it felt like the moment I met him.

My world tilted. Nothing made sense any more.

I only know he became like a drug to me... and I shook with need till my next fix.

∾

Join Alta's Facebook Group for Readers for access to deleted scenes, to chat with me and other fans and also get access to exclusive giveaways:

Alta's Private Facebook Room

∾

Check out Alta Hensley:
Website: www.altahensley.com
Facebook: facebook.com/AltaHensleyAuthor
Twitter: twitter.com/AltaHensley
Instagram: instagram.com/altahensley
BookBub: bookbub.com/authors/alta-hensley
Sign up for Alta's Newsletter: readerlinks.com/l/727720/nl